OFFSIDE

May 2001

With best wishes,

Cathy Beveridge

OFFSIDE

Cathy Beveridge

THISTLEDOWN PRESS

Canadian Cataloguing in Publication Data
Beveridge, Cathy
Offside
ISBN 1-894345-25-8
I. Title.
PS8553.E897O3 2001   jC813'.6   C2001-910466-9
PZ7.B497Of 2001

Cover and book design by J. Forrie
Typeset by Thistledown Press
Printed and bound in Canada

Thistledown Press Ltd.
633 Main Street
Saskatoon, Saskatchewan, S7H 0J8

Thistledown Press gratefully acknowledges the financial assistance of
the Canada Council for the Arts, the Saskatchewan Arts Board, and the
Government of Canada through the Book Publishing Industry
Development Program for its publishing program.

ACKNOWLEDGEMENTS:

I wish to thank Susan Musgrave for her encouragement and editorial expertise. It was a privilege to work with her. I am also grateful for the help of Bruce MacLeod MD, FRCPC, emergency physician, and Ms. Danielle Elford, skating coach. In addition, I would like to acknowledge the input, support and friendship of the 1999 Sagehill Young Adult and Children's Writing Group: Kit Pearson, Martha Attema, Jo Bannatyne-Cugnet, Norma Charles, Kathleen Cook Waldron and Sheena Koops.

For my children — Julie, Michelle and Allison —
who dared to dream with me.

CHAPTER 1

I ran my finger and thumb across the last zip-lock bag, shoved it into my ski sock and nudged my bureau drawer closed. Finished for another week and nobody suspected a thing. Sweeping my hand through the thin stream of light on the desktop, I checked my fingers for telltale powder streaks and clicked off the lamp. Then I burrowed back into bed, glanced at my alarm clock and groaned. Quarter to eleven and a 6:30 practice tomorrow morning.

Downstairs, the volume of the TV suddenly increased as a commercial interrupted the news. "Stuffed up and sneezy? The solution's easy . . . " I winced at the catchy slogan of Lise's favourite cold remedy and mimicked the commercial. "Stuffed up and sneezy? The solution's easy. Doesn't matter if you're young or old. Just mix up Sinus Minus and throw away your shyness. For a healthy sinus, minus the cold." I pulled my pillow down squarely over my head.

That was how it had all started. Some muscle-bound musician, who had probably never been stuffed up in his life, had hooked my stepmom, Lise, on Sinus Minus. From that day on, lime-green boxes in the shape of enormous noses had begun appearing in the medicine cabinets. Inside each enormous nose were ten shiny foil packets adorned with the Sinus Minus schnoz. One small sniffle was enough to elicit some serious advice to mix it with something warm for the throat. It was definitely one of Lise's latest crazes, but at least she hadn't decided to market the stuff — that was my department. In just six weeks, I'd managed to get my entire hockey team hooked on Sinus Minus.

I hadn't intended to. In fact the notion had never even entered my head before that night in October. The guys had decided to get together at Pete's for a little party while his folks were out of town. Nothing crazy, but a few of the girls had agreed to come along and I'd heard Valerie might be there.

Lise had already agreed to drop me off at Ryan's so we could walk over to Pete's, but when I came downstairs, I found her in the kitchen, running her fingers through her hair. It was red today, with a slight purple tinge, which matched her violet shirt, which didn't match her yellow vest. She was standing knee-deep in shoeboxes. Every month it was a new hair colour and a new commodity to market. Retail therapy, she called it.

"What's all this?" I queried. "Rob a shoe store today?"

Lise spread her arms wide. "This," she remarked, "is the solution to tired toes." Lise extracted a tan and navy pump from one box and a red lace-up from another.

"Does this solution have a name?"

Lise smiled proudly. "This is Calgary's first collection of Reviveets." She launched into her sales pitch. "Every woman who ever marched between towering offices or wandered aimlessly through a shopping mall must have a pair of these." She held the two clashing shoes out towards me.

"Naw, too tame," I teased. "I think you should go back to selling ironing board covers."

Lise smirked at me. The ironing board covers, depicting nude male models, had been one of Lise's few successes — until the women had used them and various parts of the male anatomy had transferred to their husbands' shirts.

Lise replaced the shoes in their respective boxes. "You laugh, Joel, but this is different." She turned the shoe to display a small latch on the heel. The heel opened to reveal a battery. "This is the first ever battery-operated shoe to massage tired feet." She pressed a button on the sole of the shoe and the entire shoe began to shake.

"Vibrating shoes!"

Lise turned the shoe off. "This, Joel Swystun, is a marketable product! You men may not appreciate it, but all the poor working women who also run a home, and who are on their feet all day long, will." She looked down at her feet. "Including me." Then she paused and smiled weakly. "How would you like to take these downstairs for me. Just store them over by — "

" — the four hundred boxes of Fibrefran, the thirty-seven cases of Hair Blush and the twenty-five bags of Lipstuck."

Lise pouted. "Joel you know those others weren't the same. Besides these Reviveets are — "

"Save it for the customers," I said, wrapping my arms around a stack of boxes. I clomped down the stairs marvelling at Lise and her schemes. "Reviveets," I muttered, stacking the boxes in the crawl space. Well, at least this was better than finding dozens of styrofoam diapers drying on the deck every day.

I traipsed back up for the second load. And anything was better than Fiberfran — "the invisible fiber supplement". Lise had added it to everything, including our ice cream, until Dad had finally forbidden her to touch the stuff. I'd never heard Dad's story, but I guessed I wasn't the only one to visit the men's room twenty-four times in one day. By the time I'd stacked all twenty boxes, I found myself asking the question I always asked.

What did Dad see in Lise anyway? Whatever it was, it was as invisible as the Fibrefran.

Lise was already waiting for me in the car. "Is brush a four letter word?" she asked, surveying my unruly mop of hair.

I flattened the haphazard black waves against my head. "At least mine doesn't change colour every month."

Lise ignored me and made the usual inquiries about the party. I found myself wishing I was sixteen and old enough to drive. Another year seemed like an eternity. Just as she got to the part about the girls, I started to sneeze. Lise looked suspiciously at me. "When did this start?"

"Must be allergic to those Reviveets," I sniffed.

We pulled into the Davis' driveway and Lise dug into her purse. "Here," she said, crinkling something into my hand. "Take them with something warm."

"What are they?" I asked, squinting in the dark.

"Sinus Minus."

"Should have guessed." I slid out of the car. "We'll walk home," I said, stuffing the foil packets into my pocket and hustling up the driveway.

Ryan threw the door open as soon as I knocked. "Where have you been? I thought you weren't coming."

I stared at my best friend. "S-oor-ry," I said in exaggerated sorrow. "I had to move two dozen boxes of vibrating shoes downstairs for Lise before I could go."

"Not again!" He shoved his feet into his open hi-tops and grabbed his team jacket off the chair. "Bye Dad."

"Bye boys. Don't be too late tonight, Ryan. That English has to be done before the hockey game tomorrow, so you can't sleep 'til noon."

"Yeah, yeah, yeah," muttered Ryan under his breath, closing the door behind him and striding down the street. I fell into step beside him, the white FALCONS on Ryan's jacket glinting in the streetlights.

"What English have you got?" I asked, wondering if I'd forgotten some important assignment.

"You know that nature story we had to do."

"Geez Ryan, that was due two weeks ago."

"I know, but McConnel sent it back for a rewrite."

That was a tough break. McConnel didn't do that sort of stuff unless it was really bad. School didn't come easily for Ryan, not like sports did. "That shouldn't take very long," I added, trying to sound encouraging.

Ryan kicked at a stone in front of him. I studied him out of the corner of my eye. There was something ruffling the Davis composure tonight and I had a feeling it was more than the English. I tried to lighten things up. "You really ought to come and see Lise's newest craze — battery-operated shoes that massage the feet."

Ryan's lips curled upwards slightly, but there were none of his usual witty comments.

"Mom's going back in tomorrow."

"Aw, geez, Ryan. Not again." Ryan's mom was a manic-depressive and in the last year she'd been in and out of the hospital quite a few times. "How long will she be gone?" I asked softly.

Ryan's shoulders shrugged beneath his jacket. "Who knows? I guess until she gets better. If she gets better." We walked on in silence and turned onto Pete's street.

"Still feel like going?" I asked. "We could just go for pizza or something instead."

Ryan thought for a minute. "Naw, I'm all right."

I followed Ryan up the driveway thinking that the party would be good for him. He could have a few games of pool, joke around with the guys and relax a bit. It couldn't be much fun at his house these days.

Ryan rang the doorbell as a car pulled into the driveway. I peered around the corner trying to see who had driven up.

"Well, are you going to come in or not?" Valerie stood behind the open door, twisting the deadbolt back and forth. Her hair hung loosely to her waist.

I stepped onto the mat, caught my trailing foot and landed face-first in the pile of shoes. Valerie erupted into laughter. By the time I had disentangled myself, the doorbell had rung again and Valerie, who was obviously on door-duty, was staring into the eyes of Rick Steiner.

"What are you doing here?" she asked. "You don't play for the Falcons anymore."

Steiner sailed through the door. "Well hello, Valerie," he said, picking up a strand of her hair and laying it gently across her bare neck. "Aren't you looking sexier than ever."

Valerie tossed her hair back just as Pete, Ryan, and Adrian came round the corner looking for me. "Hey Swystun," they called, "how about a game . . . " Their voices trailed off at the sight of Steiner, his buddy and a couple of girls I'd never seen before.

"Steiner," Adrian began uncertainly.

"Hey guys, good to see you again. It's been a while."

"That's what happens when you do time," muttered Valerie, pushing past Pete and reminding us all of Steiner's past.

"When did you get out?" asked Pete, in an unusual show of bravery.

"A while back." Steiner handed a paper bag to Pete. "I brought you a little something." Pete took the bag and we could hear the clinking of bottles.

"What else did you bring?" snapped a voice in the back.

Steiner stared at the faces of the guys he had played hockey with for the past few years and held up his arms in an innocent gesture. "Just thought I'd check in with a few old friends, but hey, if you're not cool with that, Pete, just say the word."

Pete stood awkwardly holding the bottles while all eyes turned on him. "Aw, come on in," he said finally. Then he held up the paper bag. "Why doesn't everyone have a drink."

Pete turned and swept the crowd ahead of him into the kitchen. I watched Ryan step back into the games room as Steiner passed, then moved quickly over beside him. "You want to go?" I whispered.

Ryan stood watching the guys move into the kitchen. "No," he said finally, "I'll be all right." He brushed past me and joined the crowd. A bad feeling took hold of my stomach and I wondered about clearing out right then and there. But how could I desert my best buddy now? Just as I was about to join the kitchen party, Adrian appeared in the hallway, his jacket slung across his shoulder.

"I'm out of here," he said quietly. "I don't need any more trouble." He punched his hands through his jacket sleeves. "And if I were you, I'd get Ryan out of here as well."

"He won't go. He says he can handle it."

Adrian opened the front door. "Yeah, well that's what he said last time, too. That's what we both said last time." Then the door thudded shut behind him.

"He does have a point."

I turned at the sound of Valerie's voice. "I know," I admitted, "but what am I supposed to do, drag him out of here? Besides, Steiner may even be clean."

"Yeah, right," she said, before heading in the direction of the games room.

Annoyed, I set off to find Ryan. Valerie did have a point, but Ryan had been through a lot since last April. Drugs weren't something the team did, especially not if you played for Coach Knowles. He'd spelled that out nice and clear at the start of the season and possession of any kind of a "banned substance", as he called them, meant an immediate dismissal from the team. Steiner had had a reputation for doing drugs, but nobody, including me, had known that he'd introduced Ryan and Adrian to E — those little pills that guaranteed temporary happiness. I'd found out all about it after the fact.

It had happened after Ryan's mom's first suicide attempt. Ryan's game had gone downhill with all the stuff going on at home and Coach Knowles had been threatening to drop him to second string. That's when Steiner had moved onto the scene. One afternoon before a playoff game the cops had moved in on them. Luckily, only Steiner had been buying. But Ryan and Adrian had been hauled off to the station anyway. The dealer got trafficking, Steiner was charged with possession and Ryan and Adrian were released into their parents' custody. Steiner had done time in a juvenile treatment centre.

According to Adrian, he and Ryan had only ever taken a few hits, but that hadn't stopped Ryan's dad from grounding him until the summer and then sending him to a sports camp for six weeks just to keep him busy. Ryan had never talked about it, but I was pretty sure that he'd changed his mind about using drugs.

I found Ryan twirling a pool cue in the games room. He was wearing that crazy grin he always had when he'd scored a few goals or had a drink. I watched him from the doorway. He'd be all right, I told myself. He wasn't going to get messed up with Steiner and jeopardize his hockey career again.

Ryan broke, putting three balls in the pocket. Steiner let out a cheer and held up his glass. Ryan joined him in a drink while I fretted. Ryan hardly ever drank, especially the night before a game.

The party was in full swing when I noticed that Ryan had disappeared, and so had Steiner. I made an immediate exit. Steiner was downstairs in the rec room, but Ryan was nowhere to be seen. I ran into him at the top of the stairs.

"You don't want to go down there," I told him, grabbing his arm.

He pulled free of my hold and lost his balance. "Why not? Why don't you join us?"

"Come on, Ryan," I urged. "You don't need this."

He leaned forward and I could smell the whiskey on his breath. "Yeah, maybe I do."

I blocked his way. "But you're crazy to get mixed up with Steiner. He's got a record now."

He tried to step around me. I stepped back in front of him, my mind racing as the music pulsed overhead. I tried to buy some time until I could think of what to do. "Besides, I've heard that his stuff is junk anyway."

Ryan turned back to face me.

"Impurities," I said quickly, trying to sound convincing.

Ryan looked suspiciously at me. "When did you get to know so much?"

"Angie told me," I said, grasping at straws.

"Angie, as in your sister?"

I nodded. At least he was still standing on the steps. "Everyone does it at university," I lied, "even Angie."

Ryan came back up the steps until he was standing beside me. "Angie does drugs at university?" he asked incredulously. She was hardly the druggie type.

I nodded again. "Everyone does."

Ryan started back down. "Well, Swystun, I'll never make it to university, so I won't have to worry about that."

I shoved my hands in my pockets and tried desperately to think of something else to say. My fingers wrapped around the Sinus Minus packets. "She even gave me some stuff to try last time she was home," I blurted out. Ryan froze in his tracks and looked back at me over his shoulder. I lowered my voice. "I brought it along. What do you say we try it out?"

He studied me thoughtfully for a minute. "All right," he said.

I sent Ryan off to find our coats, and grabbed a few bottles of Coke from the kitchen. We walked out onto the back deck. I looked nervously around and then dumped the contents of one package in each bottle while Ryan went to shut the back door. I swirled the Coke around and handed it to him. He looked confused. "What is it?"

"Don't know," I told him. "Angie didn't say. Just told me it was good stuff."

"I've never seen anything like it."

I swallowed hard. "It's a sports drug," I added quickly. "Some guys drink it with Gatorade."

"Performance-enhancing?" The word was a thundering whisper in the night air.

"Sure," I said, raising my bottle and picturing the Sinus Minus packet in the medicine cabinet. "It's supposed to last 24 hours."

"Well, here's to Angie." Ryan clinked his bottle against mine and took a sip.

I did the same, uncomfortably aware of the faint lemon taste on the rim of the bottle. "It's supposed to keep your head clear, keep you focused." I laughed nervously.

Ryan took another sip and wrinkled his nose.

"Guaranteed to make your aches and pains disappear," I babbled. Ryan grinned at me. "Not to mention your sinus congestion, headaches and runny nose." He laughed. "And combined with alcohol, you get a real good buzz," I added, recalling the warning on the lime green box. I almost giggled as Ryan raised his bottle again. He'd bought my story and I'd kept him out of the basement.

Ryan surveyed the dark contents of his bottle. "When's this stuff hit you?"

"Ten minutes," I said, mentally reading the writing on the side of the giant nose. "Just wait."

"I thought you'd never used it before?"

I sobered my voice. "Uh, I haven't, but Angie says . . . "

"What's Angie doing using performance-enhancing drugs anyway?"

I bit my tongue. My 45 kg sister was hardly an athlete. "She has to climb lots of steps to get to the dormitory," I said, chuckling. Ryan's crazy grin had returned.

"She must be on the second floor," he added sarcastically.

"At the end of the hall."

"A long way from the bathrooms."

I snorted loudly and Ryan doubled over with laughter.

He tried to talk. "And you ought to see how tough it is to turn on the showers. Gotta' do drugs just to stay clean."

I leaned over the railing laughing. "Pretty soon she'll be leaping from dorm to dorm in a single bound." I bounded over the railing onto the grass.

"Playing Tarzan?" asked Neal's voice behind me. I looked towards the back door at the shadowy figures of Neal and Justin, two of the guys on the team. How long had they been standing there and how much had they heard?

"Me Tarzan, him Jane," I exclaimed, pointing to Ryan.

"What are you guys doing out here anyway?" asked Neal.

I looked expectantly at Ryan. "Cartwheels!" I exclaimed, setting my bottle down and turning a mediocre cartwheel.

"That was pitiful, Swystun," said Ryan.

I got to my feet and smirked at him. "And I suppose you intend to show us how its done, eh?"

Ryan shrugged.

"And certainly not just a mere cartwheel," I announced to Justin and Neal. "But . . . an aerial cartwheel, perhaps?"

Justin snickered.

"And surely you can do it with your Coke in hand," I added.

Ryan stared at me, a slow smile crossing his face.

"I'd like to see that," said Neal.

"Which is why I am about to execute an aerial cartwheel without spilling my drink." Ryan's voice swirled around my ears.

Neal let out a murmur and disappeared inside. Justin eyed Ryan skeptically as Ryan removed his jacket in a dramatic gesture. He threw it into my arms and ignored my incredulous look. A group of curious onlookers, roused by Neal, had gathered on the back porch. I looked from the group to Ryan, who was standing on the lawn, concentrating, his Coke in hand.

He turned slowly to face me. "Well, aren't you going to give the act an intro?"

I licked my lips nervously. "Are you really going — "

"Intro please," he repeated.

I threw him one last glance and turned to face the throng on the porch. "Ladies and gentlemen, I now present to you, Riveting Ryan." I paused while Ryan bowed and the crowd clapped, their applause rippling with laughter. "For your entertainment, Riveting Ry will now execute a daring aerial cartwheel without spilling a drop."

The crowd "aahhed" on cue as Ryan held up the bottle.

"Silence please!" I commanded, and a hush fell over the throng.

Ryan held his drink in front of him and stretched up on his toes. I gulped as he ran a few steps, then threw himself upside down in a perfect aerial, landing solidly on his feet, drink intact.

The crowd exploded into applause, but I was too shocked to clap. "Encore, encore," they chorused. Ryan sipped his Coke and looked expectantly in my direction.

I threw him an admiring look. When had he become such a good gymnast? I returned to my role. "And now ladies and gentlemen, while Riveting Ry prepares for his next trick . . . " I paused, fixing my eyes on Ryan, " . . . a round-off followed by a back hand-spring, I will entertain you with a show of incredible coordination." Ryan laughed and finished his Coke.

I carried on. "Without using my hands, I will balance on one leg and drink my Coke." The crowd heckled me. "But first, I need an assistant." I grabbed Valerie's hand and pulled her down the steps. "Would you please hold the bottle." She smiled broadly and I felt my heart soar. Dramatically, I balanced on one leg, leaned forward to grasp the top of the bottle between my teeth and tipped it back, swallowing furiously. The Coke fizzed up into my nose, I sputtered helplessly and the crowd showed its appreciation. I took Valerie's hand and bowed all around.

Then I turned back to Ryan. He rolled his eyes at me. "Riveting Ry, are you ready to execute your round-off back handspring?" Ryan nodded slowly and set his empty bottle down on the grass. I stepped back beside Valerie to make room. He raised himself up on his toes, ran a few steps into a round-off and then effortlessly sailed into a back hand-spring.

"Wow!" This time I clapped too. Valerie regarded me curiously. "I didn't know he could do those," I explained quickly.

She smiled at me. "And I didn't know you were so funny."

I blushed and stepped back into my ring-master role. And so it continued, with me and Valerie doing dinky tricks while Ryan pulled off move after move.

When the show was over, Ryan plunked down on the steps beside me and the crowd went inside to warm up. "Where'd you learn to fly?" I asked, already knowing the answer.

"When did you turn into such a ham?" he retorted.

I shrugged. "Must be the stuff," I said, fingering the foil packets in my pocket. "Boy, I can hardly wait to see us on the ice tomorrow."

"Yeah," Ryan said softly, "but right now I'm wiped."

"Me too," I yawned, recalling the warning on the side of the Sinus Minus package. *Caution: May cause drowsiness.*

CHAPTER 2

Maybe it was the good night's rest, or maybe we were still on a popularity high from the night before, but we were unbeatable on the ice the next day. Ryan and I combined for five points and skated circles around our opponents. Everything would have been perfect if Neal and Justin hadn't cornered us after the game.

We were just coming out of the dressing room when they stepped out from behind the bleachers and blocked our path. "That was quite the game you two had," said Neal.

"Thanks," said Ryan.

"Rather coincidental isn't it?" asked Justin.

I glanced sideways, suddenly remembering the shadows in the doorway the night before. "I don't get it," I said.

"Yeah," drawled Neal. "I think you do." I shifted nervously as Neal stared at Ryan. "What is it, Davis? Hard stuff?"

I jumped in before Ryan could answer. "No, no, nothing like that." Ryan watched me carefully. "I mean, it's nothing illegal or anything. Well, not illegal like illegal, illegal." I struggled for the right words. "What I mean is that it's all right, uh, usually, but, uh, well it's probably not all right with Knowles or anything."

Justin looked confused.

"Performance-enhancing," whispered Ryan.

"But it's not illegal?"

I shook my head. After all, that was the truth. How could I tell Justin and Neal the real story with Ryan standing beside me?

Justin dug into his back pocket for his wallet. "Then I want in," he said decisively.

"Me too," said Neal digging out his money.

I scratched my head. "Well, I'm not sure if that's possible."

Neal leaned forward. "Come on, Swystun. We want in."

A wave of panic swept over me and Ryan shuffled nervously beside me. "Maybe Angie can get a little extra," I muttered, swallowing hard. "Look, I'll try, but I can't promise anything."

Justin and Neal shoved the money towards me. "Try hard," muttered Justin.

After they'd left, I studied Ryan. I debated about telling him the whole truth right then and there, but before I could open my mouth, Mr. Davis arrived to congratulate us, and I stayed silent.

And so it had started — just Ryan and me. Then just Ryan, Justin, Neal and me. Then just Ryan, Justin, Neal, Geordie, Theo and me. Then just Ryan, Justin, Neal, Geordie, Theo, Pete, Adrian and me. Then just Ryan, Justin, Neal, Geordie, Theo, Pete, Adrian, Scott, Dave, Jared and me. Then somehow the word got round to the rest of the team. It wasn't all that surprising — the Falcons were a pretty close-knit bunch. The incredible thing was that the guys played like champions after a dose of Sinus Minus. By the end of November we were in first place and Coach Knowles was ecstatic. The whole team was ecstatic, except for me.

I contemplated the pros and cons. First the pros — the team had never played better hockey. If we kept this up, we'd be city champs. Besides that, I was getting to be rather well off. I hummed the jingle. "So throw away your shyness and have a healthy sinus, minus the cold!" Maybe there was something to those claims after all. Ever since Pete's party, Valerie had seemed friendlier. And none of the guys had come down with colds since Sinus Minus had become a pre-game ritual.

Still, that whole ritual was one of the cons. At first, the guys had stopped by the house to pick up their stuff the night before the games. I'd figured it was wiser than going anywhere with a stash of little bags filled with fine, white powder. That was before Lise got suspicious, and before she tried to sell the guys Reviveets as the perfect Christmas present for their mothers, sisters and girlfriends. Then I'd decided to do up weekly packages and Pete had suggested we set up the weekly pizza meetings as a distribution point. We'd have a quick bite, discuss the upcoming games and everybody would go home with their weekly quota. The leftover money on the table was mine of course, even though I almost always sprang for the pizza. Maybe guilt was wearing me down after all.

Then there was the whole hassle of securing enough Sinus Minus for sixteen guys every week. The cashiers in seven different drugstores knew me by name. Even disposing of those ominous, green-nose boxes had become a problem. And of course, there was the whole question of having hooked the entire hockey team on a drug, albeit a legal, over-the-counter drug. I was especially worried about Ryan, but he just showed up for his stuff like everyone else and took it home. So far, none of the parents had discovered the guys' stashes, but that was always a possibility. As well, there was the constant fear that one of the guys would recognize it one day and the question of how it would all end. It was no wonder that I found myself staring at the ceiling most nights.

In fact, the only nights I didn't study the stucco on the ceiling were the ones before our hockey games. And that was all thanks to those shiny foil packets of Sinus Minus. I suspected they didn't really have any magical qualities, but I did know that they knocked me out and anything was worth a good night's rest. Besides, I was having a fantastic season: 3 goals, 6 assists and a plus/minus average of 2 in the last 7 games. Nobody had really noticed though. They'd been too busy watching Ryan's stats soar to 8 goals, 9 assists and a plus/minus average of 6. Still, I didn't mind. I knew Ryan would have given just about anything to play professional hockey.

But it wasn't just me and Ryan who were flying. The whole team was skating faster, shooting harder and stickhandling better than we ever had before. According to Coach Knowles, we had a good chance of winning the Christmas tournament and that meant a shot at the city title. The Falcons were flying and not just on the ice.

Being on a winning team was starting to do wonders for our popularity. Despite our parents' protests, we wore our Falcons coats all the time, regardless of the temperature. Even the guys who didn't play hockey knew who we were, not to mention the girls. It was the talk of our weekly meetings and even Carl, who wasn't exactly a ladies' man, had to admit that we were hot news when someone drew a huge heart on the school doors with FALCONS in the middle. The principal wasn't impressed, but the fact that it was done with lipstick sure impressed us. There was no doubt about it; we were definitely making a name for ourselves.

Ever since Pete's party, I'd found Valerie's name running through my head more often than not. And, I got the impression that she'd been thinking about me too. I seemed to run into her in the halls a lot more lately, and she always smiled in my direction when I did see her. But as I was usually in the midst of the team and she was usually surrounded by friends, we didn't do much more than smile at each other. Still it was a start.

"If I could just see her alone sometime long enough to talk to her," I complained to Ryan. "Then I could make an impression on her, maybe even ask her out."

Ryan laughed. "Ask her out? To where — a hockey game?"

I thought about that as Ryan pulled open the arena doors. Between practices, games, weekly meetings and exams, I didn't have a whole lot of free time. "I could ask her to the Christmas dance." The dance was coming up in a few weeks' time and some of the guys already had dates.

"Yeah right!" Ryan swung his hockey bag through the second set of doors and held the door with his foot. "She'd have to run you over before you'd ask her out."

I followed Ryan into the arena. He'd obviously seen me in action with the opposite sex before. The lobby was empty. Dad had dropped us off early. We headed toward the office to check out the dressing room assignments.

"It's just so hard to talk to her when she's with all these girls. If I had a class with her, or could arrange to see her on her own sometime — then, then I'd do it."

"Woowee!" Ryan was staring out onto the ice where a group of girls dressed in matching gold skating skirts and tight black bodysuits were lined up across the arena, their arms linked behind each other's backs. Music started and the girls began to move in perfect unison. There must have been twenty of them, but they all managed to do the same thing at the same time, going in circles, criss-crossing between lines and covering the entire ice surface in groups of five, ten, fifteen or even twenty. Ryan and I watched in amazement until the program was done.

"They're pretty good," I said. The doors swung open and the Zamboni puffed out a cloud of smoke as the girls skated off the ice.

"Hmm," grinned Ryan. "What dressing room did you say we were in?"

"I dare you." I could just imagine Ryan strolling into a dressing room with twenty girls changing.

He swung his hockey bag over his shoulder. "Never dare a Davis," he advised me as we climbed through the bleachers in the direction of the dressing rooms.

"You're all talk." I jumped down into the corridor behind Ryan. We paused in front of dressing room #3, listening to the blur of female voices behind it. "Well?" I said.

"It could be an honest mistake. We had #3 last time."

"You first. I'll be right behind . . . Valerie!" I stammered as the door burst open and Valerie rushed out and ran right into me.

"Joel, Ryan, Joel," she exclaimed looking from me to Ryan and back to me again. She still wore her black bodysuit, but had pulled a pair of jeans on over top. She stood clutching her skating bag while I stared. Her long hair had been swept up on top of her head in some sort of braid. Her eyes were blackened heavily with mascara, her cheeks a deep maroon and her lips a furious scarlet. The girls at school wore makeup, but not like this.

Her hand went to her face. "It was a dress rehearsal," she explained. "It's all part of the costume." She chewed on her scarlet lips. "Mom's waiting. Um, uh, I've got to go." She brushed past me.

"Well done, sport," Ryan said cynically as soon as Valerie was out of sight. "I'd say you charmed her all right." He exploded into laughter and pulled the door of dressing room #4 open.

I followed him in and threw my bag down under the bench. "Aw, come on, Ry, what was I supposed to do — her looking like some — "

"Hey guys. You two know the place is swarming with females?" Alex was standing in the doorway with Pete.

"Members of some synchronized skating team," added Pete.

"Yeah, yeah, we know," Ryan said, raising his eyebrows at me. "Joel's just been asking one of them out."

I threw an elbow pad at him as a bunch of the guys came barging in with the news. I pulled on my gear silently and thought of Valerie. I could have at least managed a hello or something. Every guy that came through the door had something new to add and by the time Coach Knowles arrived, the guys were buzzing.

"I take it you ran into the synchronized skating team?" he queried, smiling.

"Did we ever," said Ryan, throwing my elbow pad back at me.

Coach Knowles looked questioningly in my direction. "Well, how would you guys like to run into them a few more times?"

The guys erupted into hoots and hollers. Knowles raised his hand for silence. "The Minor Hockey Association has asked us if we'd play an exhibition fundraiser. They're trying to raise money for the new 'Say No to Drugs' campaign." I fidgeted. "You all know how strongly I feel about banned substances, especially banned substances and sports, and obviously they do too." I squirmed in my equipment. "So, they approached me to see if we'd be interested in playing an exhibition game against some Old-timers." He paused. "Old-timers led by Phil Keefler."

I gulped and a couple of the guys burst into exclamations. Phil Keefler was an ex-NHLer who lived here now. He'd been a star in his day, although that had been a while ago.

"He's put together a team of guys who used to play pretty good hockey. They're not all pros and some of them haven't skated for awhile, but they're keen to take on a bunch of youngsters with potential." He grinned at us. "They're going to bill it as youth vs. experience. I think it would be a good opportunity and it's for a worthy cause." His gaze travelled around the room.

"The game would just be one part of a weekend skating showcase," Knowles explained. "Some of the novice figure skating champions will do solos and the synchronized skating team you saw here tonight will perform as well. They skate for the provincial title next weekend."

I stared wide-eyed. Valerie had never even mentioned her skating before. Then again, I hardly knew her.

"The weekend's slated for late February, so with a little luck we might also be gearing up for a city championship title." He rubbed his hands together. "Most of the proceeds from the weekend will go to the 'Say No' campaign, but we can also keep a percentage for the team and . . . and I'm hoping it will cover some of the airfare costs." Our heads snapped up, but nobody asked the obvious. "We've been invited to the western US Invitational in Denver at Easter time."

No sooner were the words out of his mouth than the guys were leaping and high-fiving all over the dressing room. We'd been invited to out-of-town tournaments before, but never like this. The Denver tournament was pretty prestigious. Most of the junior teams and even some of the professional teams had scouts there. I looked at Ryan who had obviously made the realization about the same time I had. He was sitting against the wall with a dreamy look in his eyes.

Coach Knowles whistled and we settled back into our seats. "There are still lots of details to be worked out," he admitted, "and money's still going to be an issue, but once we get down there, you'd be billeted and it shouldn't be too costly." He paused. "I've called a parent meeting for next Monday. We'll know more then." He looked around the room, a slow smile crossing his lips. "Now get out there and warm up."

CHAPTER 3

Lying in bed that night, my thoughts kept jumping from Valerie to Denver to the Old-timers' game. I was almost certain that Knowles didn't suspect anything, but the whole thing was just a little ironic. The Minor Hockey Association was about to launch their "Say No" campaign using an entire hockey team addicted to Sinus Minus. What would Valerie say if she knew? The synchronized skating team may own Cover Girl, but I was pretty sure that was the extent of their involvement in pharmaceuticals. And then there was the question of Denver. We couldn't very well go through customs with all these little bags of white powder in our suitcases. I supposed it might be available in the states, but how was I going to manage the buying and distribution. The whole thing was crazy, absolutely crazy. I had to do something. Somehow I had to wean the team off Sinus Minus.

I studied the ceiling for an extra long time that night, but by the time I finally dozed off, I was none the wiser, only more exhausted. I do remember hitting the snooze button, or at least I think I do, but I certainly remember Lise shaking me. "Joel, it's 8:15. You're going to be late."

I sat up, took one look at the clock and bounded out of bed.

"I'll drop you off," Lise called from the hallway.

I doused my head under cold water and stared at my sunken eyes in the mirror, wondering if I shouldn't take a dose of Sinus Minus every night. Somehow I had to find a cure for this insomnia and it had better be before exams. Lise dropped me at the front doors of the school. "I really think you ought to try and get to bed early tonight, Joel," she said. I waved my half-eaten apple in her direction and headed to the office for a late slip.

Just as I was about to push the door, it flew open and Valerie ran smack into me. "We've got to stop running into each other like this," I said, grinning.

She stepped back into the office. "Sorry, I'm late for Health."

"Yeah, me too, English I mean." I let the door close behind me. Valerie did not try to leave. "Sleep in?"

She shook her head. "No, we had an early practice this morning and the buses were slow." She stood watching me as I filled out the late slip.

"You guys are really good." I ripped the slip in half and passed one to the secretary. "I've never seen synchronized skating before."

"So you know what it is. I thought hockey was the only thing on ice that you guys understood."

"We don't even understand that all the time," I admitted. We left the office together, having lost any urgency to get to class. "You know, I had no idea you were a skater."

"Since I was seven."

I studied her profile, her long eyelashes and glistening lips. "Coach Knowles told us that you have a shot at the provincial title."

She chewed on her bottom lip. "This weekend, but we have some real tough competition. I don't know."

We stood silently at the bottom of the steps. A thousand things ran through my head. I debated about asking her to the Christmas dance, but somehow it didn't seem like the right time. Instead, I said, "Just think, you're going to be a provincial champ next time I see you."

Valerie smiled at me, a long, genuine smile that wrapped itself around me. Then she turned and climbed the stairs.

I watched her until she was out of sight and then tried to take stock of my feelings. It wasn't like I was ecstatic or anything. I didn't feel like turning cartwheels down the hallway, but I had this incredible warm, contented feeling that stayed with me all morning.

That wonderful feeling might have lasted all day, except Ryan had some bad news for me at lunch. We were sitting in the cafeteria eating our sandwiches and drinking chocolate milk with a bunch of the Falcons. Scott and Theo were checking out a table of girls on the left. "The one in the red," said Scott glancing over his shoulder. "Now, she's hot."

Theo snickered. "Sure is," he agreed. "That's Candy Goodman." He paused for effect. "Bill Reid's girlfriend."

Scott slammed his fist on the table. "Just my luck!" Bill Reid was the centre on the senior basketball team — tall, well built and incredibly good-looking.

Justin elbowed me in the ribs. "So how 'bout you Swystun? Gonna' ask someone to the dance?"

I pondered that thought. Perhaps I should have done just that this morning. I glanced at the date on my watch. The dance was two and a half weeks away. "Maybe," I said, shrugging my shoulders. Valerie was one topic Ryan and I had managed to keep to ourselves and right now I wanted it to stay that way.

"And who might that be?" asked Justin.

I shrugged and changed the subject. "Don't forget the meeting tonight," I said. "Big game on Saturday."

"You bet," agreed Red, nodding his mane of long, red hair. "The Cadillacs are never easy."

"They're on a winning streak right now, too," Tony advised us. "Won their last ten games."

"Yeah, well so are we," retorted Jared. The Cadillacs were our archrivals. Chances are we'd face them in the city playoffs this year. They were last year's champs and fierce competitors. Everyone had something to say about them, everyone except Ryan. He sat sipping his chocolate milk, looking off into the distance.

I slid over to sit beside him. "Found yourself a hot date for the dance?" I asked, following his gaze.

Ryan squashed his milk carton. "Naw." He glanced at the rest of the guys. "Wanna' take a walk?" he asked under his breath.

We slipped away and ambled in the general direction of the gymnasium. I waited for him to spill his news, but it was a long time coming. After ten minutes of feigning interest in the intramural volleyball game, he gave me the bad news. "I can't make it to the meeting tonight," he said. I felt my body tense up. "Dad's got to go out of town."

I knew that meant that Ryan had to be home with his mom. Since she'd come home from the hospital in late October, the doctors' advice had been not to leave her home alone. Mr. Davis had hired a daytime companion for her, an older motherly-type who bustled around, doing housework and talking to Ryan's mom like she was perfectly normal. But she only worked until 5:30. After that, either Ryan or his dad had to be around.

It hadn't been easy for Ryan. His mom still had the odd good day, but usually she was a real zombie. She hardly ate and she looked like you could break her in two with your bare hands. And I hadn't heard her speak since she'd come back from the hospital. "Don't worry about it," I said reassuringly, "I'll drop the stuff off on my way to the meeting."

Ryan shook his head. "Don't bother. I'm not going to be able to make the game on Saturday either. Dad's away on business."

I stared at him. "The game?" I echoed. He was our leading goal scorer and we were playing the Cadillacs. "Can't Mrs. Hitchings come in for a few hours? It's not like it's late or anything."

"She's going to her niece's wedding."

My mind raced. We couldn't face the Cadillacs without Ryan. "What about your dad? Couldn't he get an earlier flight back?"

"He's gone until Sunday night."

I ran my hands over my face. "Geez Ry, there's got to be some way you can be there."

"We can't leave Mom with someone she doesn't know. Dad can't be there. Mrs. Hitchings can't be there. So I guess that leaves me." He leaned back against the wall, his eyes lifeless.

I slumped back beside him. "Have you told Coach Knowles yet?"

Ryan shook his head. "I'll have to call him."

I closed my eyes and tried to imagine someone else besides Ryan taking the faceoff on my line. We knew each other so well, read each other's moves with such ease. And lately, everything had been clicking like clockwork. Now, just when we had to face the Cadillacs, this had to happen. "Can't you get out of it?" I whined, feeling guilty as soon as the words were out of my mouth.

"No!" Ryan said decisively. "You guys can do without me, but she can't."

He pushed the door open and left. Of course, he couldn't get out of it. This wasn't some early morning practice we were talking about; this was his mother. I banged my head against the concrete. Sometimes I could be such an idiot!

Ryan was already gone by the time I reached my locker after school. To make matters worse, I missed the bus and had to wait twenty minutes. I was in a pretty foul mood by the time I got home and found the entire back entrance stacked full of Reviveets. I kicked my shoes off and dropped my jacket on the top of a bunch of boxes just as Lise, looking flushed and exhausted, came up the stairs with three more boxes. "There you are," she said. "I could use a strong set of arms."

"Forget it," I muttered and trudged into the kitchen.

She stared after me. "Bad day at school?"

I stuffed a cookie in my mouth, poured a glass of milk and glared at her.

She raised her eyebrows, brushed my coat off the tower of boxes with her elbow and deposited more Reviveets on the tower.

"Hey," I said, raising my voice and retrieving my jacket.

"You could try hanging it up for a change."

I waved it in her face. "And you could try getting a real job for a change." I grabbed my knapsack and jacket, stomped upstairs and flopped down onto my unmade bed. Fifteen minutes later, I opened up my Social Studies text and tried to concentrate. Downstairs, I could hear Lise shifting boxes around. I did have a valid point. She'd been through dozens of home-sell products and none of them had ever really been a success. Not that she had to work or anything. Dad made good money, but he deserved it working the hours he did. I started in on my homework and made some progress. I was still working when Lise knocked on the door.

"I've got a Block Watch meeting tonight," she called, "but I've put a casserole in the oven for you. Your dad won't be home until late. He's taking a client to dinner."

"Great," I called back, trying to keep the sarcasm out of my voice. Her casseroles were always an adventure. It wasn't that she was a bad cook, just that I never recognized anything she made. I guess Lise figured that a fifteen-year-old kid would eat almost anything. She was right.

I was just finishing up a quick plate of some linguine and pimento casserole when Lise appeared in the kitchen. She had changed into a fluorescent green and white striped blouse and I found myself hoping that the meeting was in a dark room. I rinsed my plate and stuck it in the dishwasher.

"Do you want me to drop you off?" she asked.

"Thanks," I said. "I'll just grab my jacket."

At least she didn't hold grudges. I hustled upstairs where my jacket lay, both inside pockets stuffed with zip-lock bags ready to be dispersed after the pizza had been eaten. I pulled one of them out and shifted it to my outside pocket. I grabbed a novel above my bed and raced downstairs. "Would you mind making a quick detour to Ryan's?" I asked. "It's on the way and I have to drop this book off."

Lise zipped up her coat. "Okay, want to grab that box behind you for me?" I swung around, my open jacket hitting the wall and the plastic zip-lock bag tumbling out onto the floor beside me. Lise bent down and picked it up. She ran her fingers across the top and turned it over in her hands. She held it by one corner and watched the fine, white powder slide across the clear surface. I leaned back against the wall and closed my eyes. "Maybe we'd better have a little chat first," she said.

"Honest," I said, looking her directly in the eyes, "that's the truth." We were seated at the kitchen table with an open box of Sinus Minus and my jacket between us. Lise was leafing through the plastic bags. I'd told her everything — all about Pete's party, letting the hockey team in on it, buying boxes of Sinus Minus, distributing it — everything. It was the only thing to do and, in fact, the more I told her, the more I wanted to tell. It was such a relief to share this crazy secret with someone else. And I didn't even stop there. I told her how I knew I had to wean the team off it, but didn't have the faintest idea how to do it.

Lise didn't say anything, just listened until I couldn't talk anymore. Then she re-zipped the pockets and put her coat back on. "I'm late," she said simply. She laughed. "Sinus Minus, hey? Your dad's going to hit the roof if this gets back to him."

I cringed. That was an understatement.

"Whatever you do, don't say anything to him, will you?" she continued.

I stared at her in surprise. Wasn't that my line?

She stood up and replaced Ryan's bag in my pocket. "Are you coming?"

I nodded. Surely she wasn't just going to pretend this had never happened. After all, she was the one that had given it to me in the first place. She must have read my thoughts.

"I know I used to think it was a bit of a cure-all, Joel," she said, "but this is hardly the same thing."

"I know, I know," I admitted. "But what do I do with all this stuff?"

"Give it to the guys," she said, handing the jacket to me.

I slipped into my jacket and took the box she'd lifted into my arms. "What?"

"Give it to the guys as usual tonight," she said. "I need time to think of a plan."

We drove to Ryan's in silence, but I could tell she was thinking. I leaned back against the headrest and relaxed for the first time in ages. It was great to have someone else thinking for a change.

Ryan met me at the door. I slid the bag into the book and handed both to him. "Figured I'd better drop this off tonight," I began awkwardly. "We've got another game on Tuesday." Ryan just nodded. From the doorway, I could see his mother sitting in the TV room.

Ryan pocketed the bag. "I owe you."

I glanced back at Mrs. Davis again. "Never mind," I murmured and swallowed hard. "Uh, about what I said at lunch today. I didn't mean it the way it sounded."

Ryan waved his hand. "Forget it," he said. "It's not important." But his eyes still had that same lifeless look.

"Did you call Knowles?"

"Not yet."

I stuffed my hands into my pockets and shuffled my feet. "I guess I'd better — " Just then a loud, sorrowful wailing reached my ears. Ryan turned and ran back to his mother who was now sobbing and gasping for breath. He knelt in front of her and tried to take her hand, but she continually pulled it away. I closed the front door behind me, her plaintive cries following me to Lise's car.

As we drove, I studied Lise out of the corner of my eye. She was definitely a little wacky, but anything had to be better than what Ryan was dealing with. He didn't say much about things at home, but I knew he wasn't looking forward to Christmas. It was the hockey that kept him going — the thrill of blasting the puck and seeing the light go on. The possibility, no matter how slim, of being scouted and making it to the big leagues someday.

Lise dropped me off at the pizza place. "We'll talk tomorrow," she said as I scrambled out of the car. I nodded, glad to have finally found a confidante, even if she was an unlikely choice.

And talk we did. Lise asked a lot of questions, even some that I'd never really thought about, like who were the leaders on the team, both on and off the ice.

"Well, Neal's the official captain, but it's Ryan that we all look to out on the ice when we're down," I said.

"And off the ice?"

"Don't know really. Scott's definitely got a way with the girls, but Pete's the social organizer. The weekly meetings were his idea. And I suppose that lately, I've been pretty influential because of the stuff."

"And you said ever since the team started taking the Sinus Minus, they've played brilliantly?"

"Yeah." I laughed. "I know it's crazy, but it's true."

"Do you take it?"

I could feel the colour creep into my face.

"But Coach Knowles doesn't know?"

"No way," I said. "He'd suspend the whole lot of us if he did."

"And these guys honestly believe it makes a difference?"

I nodded.

"Do you?" asked Lise.

I avoided her eyes. How could cold medicine be performance enhancing? And yet, I'd played so well this season. "I know that it probably doesn't really do anything except maybe make you sleep better, but it does make a difference with the guys, Lise." I struggled to explain. "It's like we've got this big secret, some sort of special ritual or something that pulls the team together. When we're on Sinus Minus, we just seem to click. We just know where the pass is going to be, what play the other guy's going to make, where to be and when."

"Hockey players have a reputation for being superstitious," admitted Lise.

I thought of James freaking out at the sight of the crossed sticks in the dressing room before the last game and how Ryan always insisted on being the last player on the ice. "Maybe that's what it is. I can't explain exactly."

Lise swirled her coffee. "And if you tried to do away with it? Say if your supply just dried up."

I grimaced. "I've thought about that. But what if the guys fall apart? We're coming up to the Christmas tournament and then there's this Old-timers' game, not to mention the Denver tournament."

"Denver? Who said anything about Denver?"

"Coach Knowles. We've been invited to the Denver tourney at Easter. It's an invitation-only tournament and it's kind of like *the* tournament of the year." I paused. "I think you'll hear about it at the meeting on Monday."

"Oh yes, Steve said something about that." Lise drained her coffee cup. "And what's all this about an Old-timers' game?"

"It's a game we're supposed to play against some old professional hockey players. Part of a skating show to raise money for the 'Say No to Drugs' campaign."

Lise rolled her eyes.

"I know," I continued. "Just a little ironic, hey?"

She nodded. "Anything else you haven't told me?"

"Naw, I think that's it. Except that I'm really worried about Ryan being back on drugs, especially with his mom the way she is now."

"Mmm, Steve mentioned that. Is she worse?"

I thought about the last time I'd seen her, Ryan kneeling at her feet, his mother sobbing. "I think so. He never really says much about her."

"And he takes the Sinus Minus too?"

I nodded, feeling terribly guilty. "We've got to do something, Lise."

She leaned back in her chair. "I know Joel," she said seriously. "And the first thing you've got to do is stop taking this stuff."

I hesitated, wondering if it would hurt my game.

Lise scowled at me.

"Okay," I agreed. "But what about the other guys?"

Lise stared off into the distance. "The way I see it, either the guys have to have a reason to want to get off this stuff, or something has to replace Sinus Minus."

"Another drug?"

"No, something else. Some other ritual or good luck charm that makes you guys a more cohesive team."

"Sounds good to me, but what?"

"That," said Lise, rising to her feet, "is the question." She deposited her mug in the sink and left the kitchen.

I watched her go, wondering if she had an

answer. I didn't think so, at least not yet. But somehow I had this odd confidence in her ability to come up with a solution. Whatever her idea was, it was bound to be original.

CHAPTER 4

Dad drove me to the game on Saturday. It was quiet in the dressing room and I knew the guys were wondering how it was going to be taking on the Cadillacs without Ryan. I was wondering too. Neal was dressed first and pacing around the dressing room. "We'll just have to pick up the slack," he said, trying to sound convincing. "Ryan's not the only one with a good shot and Joel and the rest of the wingers can still feed the centres." We nodded, but with little enthusiasm. Neal glanced once towards the door and whispered, "Besides, everybody took their stuff last night, didn't they?"

The guys nodded and I looked down. I'd stopped taking it as part of my agreement with Lise.

Neal continued, "Have we ever lost a game on the stuff?"

"Never," replied Justin.

"Well then, we're not gonna' start now, are we?"

The guys murmured amongst themselves. "That's right," agreed Carl. "We've got something to prove to the Cadillacs anyway."

"All we have to do is shut down their big gun," said Neal. "Number 5, what's his name?"

At that moment, Coach Knowles burst through the door, grinning. "Good news, lads," he said. "Dan Keller's out with the flu. He's the Cadillacs' leading scorer, number 5."

Neal let out a whoop as a new wave of enthusiasm flooded the dressing room.

"Justin will centre for Joel and Dave for the first faceoff," began Knowles, "but after that I'll be mixing things up." He brought out his clipboard and launched into his pre-game strategy speech. "You forwards, you're going to be doing some double-shifting this game, so save some legs."

I watched the other forwards — Justin, Neal, Dave, Pete, Scott, Jared and Red. Picking up the slack for Ryan wasn't going to be easy, but the guys looked determined. It was like the stuff made them feel invincible or something. I gave Knowles my full attention.

We certainly seemed invincible in the first five minutes. Neal intercepted a pass, stickhandled through their defence and laid it up perfectly to Jared who blasted one point blank past the goalie. But Smithers, the Cadillacs' right-winger, took advantage of Scott's tripping penalty, deked Adrian on the blue line and found the five-hole with a nice little wrist shot. 1-1.

The play went from end to end at a frantic pace and Knowles was making line changes on the fly. We managed quite a few shots on net, but only two decent ones, and Horvath, the Cadillac's goalie, nabbed both of them with his glove hand. Geordie was solid in our net, blocking all their shots, including O'Neill's breakaway, and literally throwing himself from one side of the net to the other to prevent a wraparound goal in the last few seconds of the period. We skated for the dressing room with a 1-1 tie.

Coach Knowles glanced over the stats for the first period while we caught our breath and poured Gatorade down our throats. "It's pretty even boys and it looks like it will be right down to the buzzer," he advised us. "The ref seems a little reluctant to use his whistle, so it's going to be a matter of fitness in the end."

I could hear Dad shouting words of encouragement as we paraded out onto the ice. Usually I went on right before Ryan, but tonight I was the last one out.

I took a few warm-up laps and then skated to my place on the centre line. Coach Knowles had been right. The referee let the play go on whenever possible and except for the odd offside and icing call, we just kept on skating end to end.

About three quarters of the way through the second period, Smithers brought me down with a stick around the knees. The crowd screamed for a penalty and got it. Neal, Dave and I were out for the power play, did some fancy passing in their zone before I put a quick wrist shot into the top stick-side corner. We were up 2-1.

It was the big break we needed. The momentum started to shift. We got three more shots away quickly and only some brilliant goaltending kept the Cadillacs in the game. That's when things started to get a little chippy. A check with an elbow thrown in, or the stick carried a little high on a skate-by. The guys were complaining on the bench, but the referee was turning a blind eye. I guess he figured there were only a few minutes left to go in the period, so why get whistle-happy at that late stage.

With just seconds to go, Neal went into the corner behind the Cadillacs' goal with one of their big defencemen, a guy nicknamed Renegade. Renegade checked Neal hard. He went down but managed to freeze the puck. The whistled sounded just as the buzzer signalled the end of the period.

Dave and I skated towards Neal. Renegade and their other defencemen were uttering ugly threats. Neal pushed them away and took off his helmet. He was bleeding just above his eye where his cage had come unhooked and cut into him. Dave skated in just as Renegade stuck his face in Neal's and I could tell that tempers were running high. So could the linesmen who promptly sent us all to our dressing rooms.

Coach Knowles cleaned Neal's cut and put some pressure on it to stop the bleeding. "It's not so bad," he said reassuringly. "Head wounds always bleed a lot."

"I'd like to give *him* a head wound," Neal muttered under his breath, and the guys agreed.

"It's getting a bit dirty out there," acknowledged Knowles. "They're starting to tire and it's a way to slow the game down."

"Tell me about it," said Red, rubbing his ribs. "I caught a butt end."

"Not to mention the elbows."

"And the knees."

"Why doesn't that bloody ref use that whistle?" groaned Justin.

Coach Knowles finished bandaging Neal. "Look you guys, you can't do anything about the ref, right? All you can do is keep skating. Eventually, they'll either lose their legs or the ref will have to call something." He paused and let his words sink in. "We're not going out there to throw elbows and wave sticks around. We're going out there to play hockey." I leaned my head back against the wall and wondered what Ryan was doing.

I could feel my legs in the warm-up. Knowles sent Dave, Justin and I out with Theo and Tony on defense. I was caught up in the traffic in front of the net, when Theo let a hard slapshot go from the point. It went in. Horvath was furious. He'd been completely screened. We were up 3 to 1. If we could just hang on for the rest of the period.

But our goal just seemed to energize the Cadillacs and four minutes later, their right winger, MacMillan, drove to the net and let a bullet rip. It hit Geordie in the neck and bounced back out in front of the net. The left winger tucked the rebound in behind Geordie and suddenly it was 3 to 2.

Coach Knowles called a time out. I was panting like a dog and there were still thirteen minutes to go. I poured the Gatorade in and tried to dig deep like Knowles was suggesting.

Play went end to end for the next nine minutes with only a handful of whistles. The Cadillacs won an icing faceoff in our zone and the point man opted to shoot, raising the puck just a few inches. Unfortunately Dave deflected it over Geordie's shoulder, leaving us tied, 3-3, with only a few minutes left in the game.

Halfway through my next shift, I opted for an early change. My legs were throbbing now and I found myself watching the clock, willing the seconds to tick away. Our line was waiting to change up when Scott got levelled from behind. A late hit by Renegade. We heard the crack of Scott's helmet on the ice and jumped the boards as the whistle blew.

I remember thinking that the whole thing happened in slow motion. Neal was on top of Renegade before the guy had regained his balance. The two of them went down hard in front of the goal and in seconds the other defenceman had jumped in with Pete. I could hear Knowles screaming at us to stay out, but within moments the teams had squared off. Alex and one of their wingers were half-tangled, but the rest of us were just dancing around with a Cadillac. I'd squared off with Smithers who didn't really look like he wanted a fight. I felt the same way.

The referee and linesman managed to separate Neal and Renegade. Scott was still on the ice, sitting up and looking dazed. Pete and one of the Cadillacs' defencemen were still toe-to-toe and bare-fisted having just been pried apart by a linesman. Insults were being thrown around, but the fists had stopped flying. We skated to our respective benches and waited for the ref to dish out the penalties.

Neal and Pete, along with two of the Cadillacs, were given five minute majors and game misconducts. Renegade got an extra two minutes for cross-checking. Alex and the Cadillacs' defenceman he'd tangled with got minors for roughing, and the rest of us, including Coach Knowles, were given a stern talking to about bench-clearing brawls. I thought about telling the ref that none of this would have happened if he had known what the whistle was for two periods ago, but I didn't think now was the appropriate moment.

Play resumed. For two minutes, Dave, Justin and Red went out on our man-advantage. Despite a few good opportunities, they couldn't get the puck by Horvath. Our enthusiasm seemed to be waning. The period ended without any scoring and we dragged ourselves off the ice, lucky to get away with a tie.

Coach Knowles didn't have much to say after the game. He wasn't big on fighting and he always said that only the weak lost their temper. Dad was more philosophical about the whole thing and thought an occasional fight was a good team-building exercise. I'm not sure Pete would have agreed. His eye was swollen shut and had already turned purple by the time we'd left the arena. I was just exhausted and glad it was over.

My whole body ached by the time we got home and even a hot shower didn't seem to help. Lise made me a cup of hot chocolate and said that Ryan had called three times while I was in the shower.

"At least you'll have lots to tell him," said Dad. "And you guys still haven't lost in eight games."

Ryan was ready to jump through the phone by the time I reached him. "Did you win?"

"Tied."

"At least you didn't lose." He waited. "Well?"

I wasn't sure where to begin, but I figured the beginning was a pretty good place. He was full of questions, but my head was pounding by the time we got to the third period. "Look," I said, "I gotta' go. I'm absolutely beat."

Ryan chuckled. "Serves you right for cheating on your stamina laps."

I couldn't believe that I hadn't even told him about the fight, but I hung up and dragged myself to bed. I felt like I'd been beaten to a pulp.

Dad checked in on me a few minutes later. "Hey Joel, you look like you're burning up." He put one hand on my forehead. "I'll get you some water. I bet you've got the flu, like half the office."

CHAPTER 5

By the next morning I had to agree with Dad. I spent the whole day in bed, hardly conscious of people coming and going. I was delirious with fever and my only memory was of someone trying to get me to drink. My throat burned and my head felt like it was going to explode. I took whatever pills I was given — strawberry, grape, or just plain chalk — and hoped I could keep them down. I remember screaming for the window to be opened and then, before Dad had even opened it, asking for extra blankets. The day slipped into night and finally I woke in the moonlight, feeling conscious for the first time. I propped myself up on one elbow and reached for the glass of water on the night table. My head still throbbed, and I could barely swallow. But at least the fever had subsided. I stumbled to the bathroom and crawled back to bed. The clock showed 3:34 as I drifted back to sleep.

I had just awakened when Lise poked her head into my bedroom. "Hey, Joel, how are you feeling?" She opened my blinds, the seagulls on her fuchsia sweatshirt glinting in the sun.

I rubbed my eyes. "What day is it?"

"It's Monday morning. You had a tough couple of days."

"My English is due today."

Lise laughed. "You're not going anywhere. Do you feel like you could eat? I'll bring you up something."

I ran a hand through my hair, matted with sweat. "I think I'll have a shower first."

"Okay, holler if you need anything." She disappeared around the corner and down the stairs.

I swung my legs over the side of the bed and the room began to spin, turning it into a kaleidoscope of colours. I eased myself back onto the bed. I must have fallen asleep before Lise returned with some flat ginger ale and soda crackers. They were sitting on my night table when I woke about noon. I reached for the ginger ale and took a sip. Then, having learned my lesson once already, I sat up slowly and shuffled to the bathroom. Lise obviously heard me, because she was upstairs just about the same time I crawled into my bed.

"Welcome back to the land of the living."

I sipped my ginger ale. "I'm not sure I'm there yet."

"You're certainly a lot closer than you've been the last few days."

I leaned back against my pillow and yawned. "See what happens when you don't take your Sinus Minus?"

Lise pulled a face at me. "You know it doesn't work that way, Joel."

"I know, I know," I said.

"Ryan called," she told me, "and a few of the other guys on the team. Ryan said he'd stop by tonight."

"It's Monday today, right?" I asked.

Lise nodded. "Tonight's the parents' meeting for the hockey team."

"Oh yeah, and we've got a practice tomorrow."

"You won't be skating tomorrow, Joel."

I raised my arm to protest, but my biceps ached so much that I didn't bother.

The phone rang and Lise turned to go. "I'll be downstairs if you need anything."

"Thanks," I muttered. "I think I'll just get dressed and come down."

That had been my intention, but the next thing I remember was Dad's voice drifting up the stairs. "Come on in, Ryan. I think he might be sleeping, but according to Lise he's been asleep most of the day, so it's probably a good idea to wake him so he sleeps tonight."

I rubbed my eyes and propped myself up on the pillow just as Dad and Ryan walked into the room. "Hi Dad, Ryan," I croaked.

"Feeling any better?" Dad asked.

"I think so. Geez, is it already nighttime?" The streetlights gleamed outside my window.

"I'll leave you boys and bring you up something to drink," said Dad, excusing himself.

Ryan sank into the chair beside my desk. "Swystun, you look awful."

"Thanks," I said. "Did I miss anything at school today?"

"Only all the talk about the fight the other night."

"Oh yeah, sorry about that."

Ryan waved off my apology. "Never mind, I've heard about it so many times, I feel like I was there."

"I wish you had been. We could have used you."

"You guys managed a tie."

"Only because Keller was out with the flu."

Dad brought in a flat ginger ale for me and a Coke for Ryan.

"I guess you won't be practising tomorrow, eh?" asked Ryan.

"Not likely. I feel like I've been run over by a semi." I yawned and Ryan shifted uneasily in his chair.

"Well, we've got a game against the Blades on Thursday and another one on Sunday this week," he said. He cleared his throat and whispered. "Some of the guys are wondering about the stuff for this week."

"Geez, I'd forgotten all about that."

Lise stuck her head in the doorway. "Hey Joel, feeling better?" I nodded. "We're off to the hockey meeting now. Do you want us to drop you off, Ryan?"

Ryan stood up. "Yeah, that would be great. Dad wanted to go tonight, so I've got to be home." He slapped me on the shoulder and I winced. "Take it easy, and I'll give you a call."

After they had gone, I lay back in bed and thought. There was no way I was going to be practising tomorrow, but maybe I'd be up and about in time for a weekly meeting on Wednesday. Then a thought took hold of me. If I wasn't back to health in time for the meeting, the guys wouldn't get their stuff. That had its pros and cons. The Blades were the second-last-place team in the league, Ryan would be there, and the talk would all be of Denver. It would be the perfect time to wean the guys off Sinus Minus. Just wait until I told Lise.

"Well you look much happier," said Dad, flopping down on the end of the bed a few minutes later. "But I don't expect that you'll be back at school tomorrow. The guys at work have been averaging four or five days off at a time. I just hope you don't give it to me."

I drank my ginger ale. "I thought you were going to the meeting."

"Lise and I had both planned on going, but we figured one of us had better be home with you feeling this way." He paused and looked thoughtful. "Lise was really keen to go for some reason, so . . . "

I could imagine Lise at the meeting, trying to figure out some way to help me wean the guys off the stuff. I smiled at Dad. "She's probably looking for potential Reviveets customers."

Dad smiled, but then looked serious. "I know Lise has some wild ideas from time to time and her marketing schemes can be a bit . . . unusual, but she is trying."

"I know, Dad," I said, thinking of the long conversations I'd had with Lise this past week. "She's okay."

"It isn't easy for anyone in the first few years."

The phone rang and I was saved from any further discussion as Dad went to answer it downstairs. I figured I'd stay up and see what Coach Knowles had said at the meeting, but I was asleep by the time Lise came in.

She filled me in on the meeting the next morning. I had made a half-hearted attempt to eat, but even toast wasn't sitting very well and just looking at the yogurt Lise had included on my tray made my stomach flop. I was sitting up in bed wondering if I had the energy to get up when she showed up in my doorway.

"Not much of an appetite yet?" I shook my head. "Oh well, you'll get over it eventually and go back to demolishing the refrigerator."

I passed her the tray. "How did the meeting go last night?"

"Well, Coach Knowles is pretty excited about Denver. He's not sure how much money you guys will need to get down there, but it sounds like just about everything will be taken care of once you're there. He's hoping that this skating showcase will be a big fundraiser and he asked for people to help promote and organize it." I waited. "I said I'd help out — talk to the other clubs participating and come up with some original ideas to market it." I sank down under my sheets.

She cleared her throat. "He feels pretty strongly about sports and drugs, doesn't he?"

I nodded. I could hardly wait to see Lise's reaction when I told her my plan.

"I just wish I knew what to do, Joel."

"You don't have to worry about that anymore, Lise."

She raised her eyebrows in surprise.

"I've figured it out." I let her speculate for a minute. "Our next game is on Thursday and the guys are out of stuff after tonight's game. Normally, we'd have a weekly meeting on Wednesday, but I'm sick right? If I'm not even well enough to go to school, I'm not going to be able to go to a meeting, so the guys won't get their stuff."

"And you think that will be all right?"

I shrugged. "They'll probably be a little upset at first, but think about it. First, we're playing the Blades — the second-last-place team in the league. Second, everyone's going to be fired up about Denver, including Ryan."

Lise picked up the tray again. "Sounds reasonable to me. Then you'll just have to convince them that your supply has dried up and they don't really need the stuff to win."

I rubbed my hands together and smirked. "See, coming off Sinus Minus and getting this flu was the answer."

"And you're sure the guys will win?"

"Against the Blades — we couldn't lose if we tried." Lise meandered downstairs and I snuggled back under the covers. My body still ached when I moved, but I was definitely on the mend. Nevertheless, I didn't want to mend too quickly. I couldn't go back to school before Friday.

Ryan stopped by on Wednesday with some English and Social homework. The practice had gone well and everyone, including Ryan, was excited about Denver. The scouts were sure to be there and the whole tournament, according to Knowles, was first class. His eyes lit up when he spoke about it. When both Lise and Dad had left the TV room, Ryan asked the question I was waiting for. "Some of the guys are asking about the stuff, Joel. There's still a meeting tonight, but with you being sick and all . . . " Lise strolled through to the kitchen and I looked back at the television. " . . . Pete wondered if I could bring it tonight?"

I shook my head. "I haven't had a chance to do anything with Lise and Dad hovering over me all the time," I whispered. "I'll try to bring it to the game."

Ryan clenched and unclenched his fingers. "You figure you'll be back tomorrow?"

"I think so," I lied. "Dad's not keen on me missing so much school."

Ryan grinned at me. "Oh yeah, there's someone else who doesn't seem to like you missing school either." Ryan's grin spread mischievously across his face. "Valerie's been hanging around your locker these past few days." He dug into his pocket and produced a torn bit of paper. "She asked if you'd call her."

Valerie! I had forgotten all about her big competition last weekend. I took the piece of paper with her scrawled phone number. "Did she say anything?" I asked, stuffing the paper in my pocket.

"Just asked if I knew when you'd be back."

"Her synchronized skating team skated for the provincial title this past weekend. I wonder if they won?"

"Beats me," said Ryan, rising and grabbing his jacket. "Why don't you call her and see?" He grinned that crazy Davis grin again and headed towards the doorway. "See you tomorrow maybe."

After Ryan had left, I moseyed up to the kitchen and fixed myself a sandwich. I was halfway through it and looking over my English assignment when Dad and Lise walked in.

"Hey Joel, you're looking better," beamed Dad. "Good to see your appetite back again." He smiled in Lise's direction. "You can always tell when he's better, because the refrigerator's empty." I stuffed the last of my sandwich in my mouth. "Better get after that homework — look's like you'll be back at school tomorrow."

I stopped chewing and shot a desperate look at Lise behind Dad's back. "Uh, well Steve," said Lise, "I'm not sure we should rush him back. This flu's going to leave him pretty tired and weak."

Dad popped the lid off a bottle of Coke. "Are you kidding? The way he's eating?" He took a long slurp. "Besides, exams aren't far off and Joel can't afford to miss too much now."

Lise raised her eyebrows at me as I tried to think of something. I couldn't go back to school tomorrow. The guys would be expecting me to have the stuff and then my whole plan would be shot. I thought about trying to look sick now — slap my cheeks until they were bright red, or double over in pain, but I didn't think Dad would go for it. I shrugged at Lise. About the only thing I could do was throw up the sandwich I'd just eaten and I didn't think anyone would be keen on that — least of all me.

Lise walked across and put her hand on my forehead. "He's still a little warm. One more day at home wouldn't hurt."

But Dad wasn't listening. "Nonsense. Joel's well enough to go back to school tomorrow."

There was a note of finality in his voice that I had heard too many times to argue. There was only one thing to do. "Dad's right," I said quickly, springing up out of the chair. "I'm fine. In fact, I'm starved."

"See?" said Dad to Lise who was staring incredulously at me.

I dug into the fridge and brought out an apple and the cheese. "In fact, I feel good enough to play tomorrow night."

Dad smiled in my direction. "See how you feel after a full day at school, son."

"I'll be fine, Dad. Anyway, it's only the Blades. We kicked them last time, so it shouldn't be a tough game." Lise was still looking at me like I'd lost my marbles. "Ryan'll be back and we're really hot right now. We've got this new play where Theo takes the puck in over the centre line, drops it back . . . " I babbled on, drawing haphazardly across Dad's paper with my half-eaten apple. Lise shook her head and went downstairs to take stock of her Reviveets.

I was working on my English on the dining room table the next time she went by. Dad was on the phone in the family room. "What got into you?" she whispered.

I could hear Dad hang up the phone. "You'll see," I replied.

She straightened up as Dad wandered into the room. "How's it going Joel?" I busied myself with my writing. "I was just going to make a cup of tea, Lise. Would you like one?"

She nodded and followed him into the kitchen, glancing back at me.

As soon as they had moved into the family room to watch TV and I heard the kettle singing, I dashed into the kitchen. I opened the window behind the table and stood over the kettle. Within just a few minutes, my face was hot and damp, my hair dripping. I ran a hand through my hair. "Kettle's boiling," I called. I waited until I heard Dad's footsteps. "I'll make the tea," I said, starting to cough at the end of the sentence.

By the time Dad entered the kitchen, I was already coughing hard, reaching for the mugs. "You okay, Joel?" I straightened up and then clutched my abdomen and kept coughing. In fact, the coughing had taken over and I was in a real fit. "You don't look so good. Why don't you sit down?" He led me across to the kitchen table and I eased myself into the chair in front of the open window while he went to unplug the kettle.

The coughing had aggravated my throat and my voice was husky and strained. "I'm fine, Dad. I rubbed my gut again and winced ever so slightly.

"Your stomach bothering you?"

"Not really."

Dad put a hand on my forehead. "You are still a bit hot and you're all sweaty." By this time Lise had joined us in the kitchen.

I stood up, swayed slightly and grabbed onto the table. "It's nothing, Dad, really." I could see Lise smirking at me and had to concentrate hard so as not to smile.

Dad hesitated. "I'm not so sure, Joel. Maybe Lise is right. One more day at home might see it all through."

I shook my head. "But Dad, I've already missed three days of school and we've got exams coming up." The cold winter air had replaced the warm steam and I shivered.

"Phone around and see if the guys can give Ryan the homework you've missed. You're not going to learn anything if you've got chills and fevers in school."

"But Dad," I protested, "we've got a game tomorrow and — "

"You heard me. One more day. You can go back on Friday."

I nodded meekly. "I'll go phone the guys," I said. Lise applauded silently behind Dad's back as I made my way upstairs.

I did phone a few of the guys in my classes, but I wasn't at all confident that they were going to remember the homework. Every one of them had the same concern — how were they going to play without the stuff?

"Look Neal, I'm sorry, but I just can't make it. I've got the flu." I paused as he exploded into a fury of words. "Of course I'm sure. Ask Ryan. He'll tell you. Besides, it's only the Blades and Ryan's back in the line-up. You guys will be fine." Lise stuck her head in the door. "Listen," I said, thankful for her presence, "I've got to go. Don't forget to give Ryan the Math homework, okay?"

I hung up and she slipped inside the door, closing it behind her. "How are they taking it?" she asked.

"Not well," I replied. Even I hadn't anticipated such a strong reaction to my news. "I'm not sure this is such a good idea."

"You've come this far now, Joel. You have to give it a try."

"I know," I moaned. "I just hope it works."

"Me too," said Lise. "Sometimes things work out when you least expect them to." The phone rang and I rolled my eyes. "I'll get it," she said as I fell back on the bed. It was almost certain to be one of the team wanting to know. "He is here," said Lise's voice as I groaned, "but he's still not feeling well. He's asleep right now, but I'll tell him you called."

I grinned up at the ceiling. "Thanks," I said as Lise put the receiver down.

"I turned off your ringer. I'll take all the calls downstairs." She made her way to the door, in a sort of bouncy way.

"Why are you walking so funny?" I asked.

"Reviveets," she said. "They make your feet feel so sproingy."

I lay back on the bed and laughed. Lise was okay, a little weird maybe, but okay.

I could hear the phone ringing all evening long. The whole thing had gotten completely out of control. I couldn't concentrate to read. Tomorrow the guys would have to play their first game in months without Sinus Minus. I tried to imagine the quiet discontent in the dressing room — Coach Knowles would be wondering what was going on. And Ryan, how would he be? He hadn't said much so far. But then again, he was going to bring the homework tomorrow after school. What if he hit me up for it then? I stewed about it for a long time, the phone ringing every few minutes downstairs. At 9:40, I collapsed into bed thinking that we must have had a record number of phone calls. PHONE CALLS! Oh no! I'd forgotten to call Valerie. I glanced at the clock. It was too late now. What was she going to think of me? I might be on my way to improving the situation with the hockey team, but I certainly wasn't improving my chances with Valerie.

CHAPTER 6

I moped around the house all the next day until Lise finally told me to take the dog out for a walk. Jasper was busy digging up the backyard when I whistled for him and he came bounding. His thick fur was wet from rolling in the dirt and snow and I wondered if we'd have a white Christmas this year. It was one of my favourite seasons. Angie would be home for more than just a passing night or two and Dad always took a week or so off. When I was younger, we used to go tobogganing and skating over the holidays. But the last few years, we'd spent our time at the hockey rinks.

The tournament always ran between Christmas and New Year's. Angie and Dad had always come to most of my games, but Mom had never really enjoyed sitting in the arenas watching a bunch of guys scrape up the ice. She'd only seen me play a few times, and complained about how cold it had been. She'd never liked the cold — that's why she moved south when she and Dad had decided to call it quits. It had been a long time ago. I did some mental calculations: almost seven years now. I flew down to see her in the summer, but she was remarried now with little kids and it wasn't really my idea of a good time. I think she understood in a funny sort of way.

The first Christmas after she'd left, Dad had gone overboard trying to keep Angie and me entertained, and that had sort of set the trend. Angie says it was horrible — having to toboggan, swim, skate, and ski every minute of the day, but I thought it was great. I threw Jasper's ball out into the trees. Yep, Christmas was one of my favourite times.

But first I had to get through exams. The thought of school sobered me, until I remembered the Christmas dance. For the first time ever, I honestly believed I'd ask a girl to the dance. The team joked about it every year, but this year maybe Valerie would go with me. That was, of course, if she wasn't totally put off about me not calling. What were those profound words I'd said to her that day? "Next time I see you, you'll be a provincial champion?" I raced Jasper down the path, wondering if she'd won.

Lise was just leaving when I got back and left Jasper resting in the backyard. "I've got a meeting," she informed me.

"For what?"

"This skating showcase. We're trying to come up with some original marketing ideas so you guys can go to Denver." She looked thoughtful. "What do you think about having a theme for the weekend. Something like 'Hollywood on Ice' and having you guys change the names on your uniforms to movie stars. Then the girls could skate to one of the themes from Broadway and — "

"Hollywood and hockey don't have a lot in common," I told her.

She scowled at me. "Well, you're going to have to cooperate if this is going to work."

"That doesn't mean we have to go around looking like a bunch of weirdos." I pushed past her into the family room. "Next thing you know, you'll have us all dressed up in some wild costumes."

Her eyes lit up for a second as she closed the door behind her and I wondered if her getting involved with the committee was such a good idea. I finished off my homework, had a few snacks and whiled away the afternoon in front of the television. Valerie's number was folded inside my pocket and I was determined to call her just as soon as school let out. Surely she'd be sympathetic when she found out how ill I'd been. Maybe I'd even ask her to the dance. Yeah, that's what I'd do.

I was still determined when Ryan arrived laden down with my homework. "Geez," I moaned. "How am I ever going to get all this done for tomorrow?"

"You asked for it." Ryan was in good spirits. I watched him to see if he was going to bring up the subject of the stuff, but he didn't say anything, just rambled on about some of the antics in phys. ed.

Finally, I could bear it no longer. "Are the guys ready for the game tonight?" I ventured.

"Yeah, I think so. The Blades have lost their last three games and the word is that their coach is leaving, so I don't think they'll be much trouble." He opened his mouth to add something, just as Lise walked in wearing her zebra suit.

Ryan stared at the black and white zigzags of her overalls and tried not to laugh.

"Hi Ryan. I see you brought Joel's homework. Thanks a lot."

"How did the meeting go?" I asked, then explained to Ryan. "Lise signed up for the showcase committee."

"It was good," said Lise, setting down her bag of groceries and hanging up her coat. "We've got some interesting ideas that we're looking into."

I felt a deep sense of foreboding as I watched her walk into the kitchen, and wondered if Ryan was feeling the same thing.

But Ry was lost in his dreams. "Can you imagine skating on the same ice with guys like Phil Keefler? I wonder if he still wears #55?"

"We'll probably find out. I don't think we stand a chance."

Ryan frowned at me. "Of course we do. We just have to out-skate them. After all we're half their age." The dreamy look crept back into his eyes.

I think I realized at that moment how important hockey was for Ryan. Hockey was definitely a big part of my life now, but it wasn't an obsession like it was with Ryan. He ate, slept, played and dreamed the game. I guess that was why he was a cut above the rest of us.

"I've got to get home," Ryan said, slapping me on the shoulder. "It's an early game. I'll miss you out there tonight."

Here it comes, I thought. Here's where I get the request for the stuff.

"You boys want some dates stuffed with cream cheese?" called Lise. "They look delicious."

"No thanks Lise," said Ryan. "I have to go, but Joel would love some."

I kicked him as Lise brought in a plate of wrinkled black and white canoes and set them in front of me. "They're absolutely delectable," she said, licking her fingers. "Ryan, take one with you."

"That's okay," said Ryan, trying not to laugh as Lise went back to the kitchen.

"Yeah, Ryan, take one with you. In fact, take the whole plate with you," I said, mimicking Lise's high pitch as I walked him to the door.

"I'll call you after the game."

"Good luck," I yelled after him.

He stopped partway down the sidewalk and turned. "By the way, how did she do?"

"Who?"

"Valerie, you idiot. How did she do with her synchronized skating?"

"I don't know. I didn't call."

Ryan grinned. "Coward," he shouted, and ran out onto the road.

I shut the door behind me. I wasn't a coward. I just had too much on my mind these days. I clutched the paper in my pocket. But there was nothing to prevent me from calling now. I took the stairs two at a time, closed my door and took the number from my pocket. My hands were trembling as I punched the numbers. One ring, two rings, three rings — click — the answering machine. It must have been Valerie's mom's voice and it left me feeling unnerved. I hung up and tried to regain my composure. I could have left a message — asked her to call back. Never mind, I told myself, I'd call her again later. And I did, right before supper, but there was still no answer. I didn't leave a message. Better to talk to her in person, I rationalized.

I dug into my homework, wondering if this whole scheme had been such a good idea. There was a lot to catch up on, especially in Math. I looked at my watch. The guys would be partway through the game now. I wondered how it was going without the stuff. Surely it wasn't going to make any difference. It couldn't. After all it was only cold medicine. I threw myself back into my homework.

Half an hour later, I mustered my nerve and decided to call Valerie again. But Lise was on the phone downstairs. I replaced the receiver gently and tackled my English. By 8:00, I was certain she'd be home. Lise's voice laughed into my ear. I went down to get something to eat. Lise was chatting away with a long list in front of her. "Is she going to be on the phone forever?" I asked Dad, who was reading some document for work.

"Don't know, Joel. Something to do with your tournament in Denver." He wrinkled his brow. "Who do you need to call? I thought all your friends would be at the rink?"

I could feel the colour creep into my face. "It's not important," I muttered as I trudged back up the stairs.

By 8:30 I debated about asking Lise if she could rest her jaws just long enough to let me make a phone call, but I didn't want any suspicious inquiries. I kept trying to guage how long she'd be, but I kept missing the few seconds in between calls.

Ryan was luckier. He got through just after 9:30. "Hey Joel, you and Valerie set a date yet?"

"What?"

"For the wedding. I've been trying to get through for thirty-five minutes."

"It's Lise," I complained. "She's buying up shares in the telephone company." I waited, but Ryan said nothing. "Well?" I asked.

"We lost."

My head swooned and the room spun. "You what?"

"We lost. We lost to the Blades tonight."

The stuff. The guys hadn't had the stuff. "You lost to the Blades?"

"That's what I said. Five to two."

"Five to two?" I couldn't believe what I was hearing.

"Yep."

Part of me wanted to ask what had happened, but the rest of me already knew.

"Just fell apart out there," Ryan told me. "Couldn't do anything right tonight."

I thought I could hear an accusing note in his voice. I waited, expecting him to tell me how much the guys needed the Sinus Minus, how important it was to sustain our winning streak, but he didn't. "That's not going to help our standings," I said.

"Nope." There was a moment's silence.

"It's because of the stuff isn't it?" I asked in a whisper.

Ryan didn't answer at first. "Yeah Joel," he said, "maybe you should — "

"Don't worry, Ryan. I'll do it all up tonight and everyone will have it for the next game. Besides, we'll have our regular lines back by Saturday — the Panthers don't stand a chance." I tried to sound optimistic.

But Ryan didn't jump at my enthusiasm. "Yeah, I guess so," he said. "Look Joel, I've got loads of homework to do and Dad's on my case already. You coming to school tomorrow?"

"Yeah, sure, I'll be there. See you then." I put the receiver down. The guys had lost to the second-last-place team in the league who was having troubles with their coach. I couldn't believe it. The Falcons should have waxed them. I paced between my window and bed. What was happening to the team? It wasn't like you could get addicted to cold medicine, was it? And it didn't have any physical effects, other than to dry up your sinuses, did it? I'd read the labels on the Sinus Minus boxes a hundred times.

"Joel, you all done on the phone?" Lise knocked on the door.

I threw it open. "They lost. They lost tonight," I whispered violently.

She stepped inside. "The Falcons lost tonight?" I nodded. "But I thought you said they wouldn't have any trouble with the Blazes."

"Blades," I snapped. "And they shouldn't have. Ryan says they just fell apart." I spun around. "It's the stuff, Lise. They can't play without it."

"Oh come on, Joel, it's all psychological. Every team has a bad game from time to time. It happens."

"We didn't just have a bad game."

"But you weren't even there." She smiled. "Maybe they just can't win without you."

I scowled at her. "It's the stuff, Lise. They need it."

"You don't know that. I've been thinking — why don't you just tell them what it really is? Maybe they'd just think it was a big joke." She paused. "You might have to make a few refunds though."

"And take away our good luck ritual. Are you crazy?" I banged the desk. "If we start losing now, we won't even have a shot at the playoffs never mind the city championships." I glared at Lise. "I'm giving it out again. At the next team meeting." I had to. I owed it to the guys — to Ryan and all of them.

"Joel, I think you're jumping to conclusions. Why not give it another game and see how — "

"We play the Panthers on Saturday. They're one of the better teams in the league. No way, Lise, no way!" I guess I must have inherited Dad's final voice because she didn't argue with me.

"It's got to stop sometime, Joel."

I almost shouted at her. "And you said you would find a way to make that happen, so do it." I knew that hadn't been a fair remark. I sank onto my bed and stared at the stucco on my ceiling.

The guys were all over me the next day. We called a team meeting for that night and I promised them I'd deliver. I'd hardly slept the night before and between the guys and my teachers, it was one lousy day. McConnell sent my English back for a rewrite and Ward gave me some extra sheets of Math as make-up work. But the real clincher came at lunchtime. I'd been looking for Valerie all morning, but hadn't run into her. I was one of the first to reach the cafeteria and take up residence at my usual spot next to Adrian and Theo. Ryan came down a few minutes later, but sat at the other end and I thought he seemed kind of cool and distant. Geordie and Scott were talking about the Christmas dance.

"Hauk did a poll in gym today. He asked the guys in our class how many of them had dates for the dance and only five of them put up their hands," said Justin.

Tony chimed in. "I heard that Patrick Jameson asked Fiona Williams."

We laughed. "They're perfect for each other," added Alex. "They'll probably bring their matching pencil cases."

"Terry and Marlene are going of course," continued Tony.

"Of course," we sang in unison. Those two had been going out for almost two years now.

"And rumour has it," continued Tony, "that Cory Martinson's asked Valerie Sherman."

I sat staring blankly at the wall. Cory Martinson had asked Valerie. I only vaguely heard the talk around my ears. "He always goes in for the girls with long hair. Didn't he take Emma Turnbull to a dance last year?" Cory Martinson played for the Panthers. We'd never been on particularly friendly terms because of it and now he had the nerve to take Valerie to the dance. I glanced at Ryan who I was sure had heard, but he wasn't looking up. I finished my lunch and wandered up to the library to do some homework. But I spent most of the time staring out the window, wondering exactly what Valerie saw in Cory Martinson.

Just before the afternoon bell, I started downstairs to my locker. I thought I heard Valerie's voice and picked up the pace. Her long hair swished down the last flight of stairs in front of me. It would have been easy to call after her, ask her how she'd done in the provincial championships, but what was the point now? I was better off forgetting about her and concentrating on hockey.

All the guys were at the meeting that night and the mood was upbeat. Even Ryan seemed a little more relaxed when the talk turned to the game against the Panthers. I had a score to settle with Cory and tomorrow on the ice was as good a place as any to do it. The team had something to prove to Knowles and each other, too, and I was sure we'd beat the Panthers the next night. By the time we'd packed up, the guys seemed like their old selves.

"I heard what Tony said about Cory Martinson today," Ryan said as we strode out into the darkness. The wind was a biting one and I wondered how wise it had been to say we'd walk home. I turned up my collar and snapped my coat.

"Yeah, well I'll see him on the ice tomorrow."

"You didn't call Valerie?" It was a cross between a statement and a question and I let it go, concentrating instead on the crunch of our shoes over the snow. "You still want to go?"

"To the dance?" I thought about that for a while. Valerie wasn't the only girl in the school. "Yeah, why not. How about you?" Ryan never talked about girls much. In fact he never talked about anything much except hockey.

"Sure, it's a good out."

I slid across some black ice and my sneakers hit the pavement with a thud on the other side. "How is your mom?"

"About the same, I guess." He sighed. "Some days she's good. Some days, well, some days you don't want to live there."

We were almost at the intersection where we parted ways. "Dad said he'd pick you up for the game," I said.

Ryan waved and broke into a jog. It was getting cold now and there was snow forecast for the whole weekend.

In fact, it snowed so much that Angie didn't get home for the weekend as she'd planned. I had my nose in my books trying to get caught up and was out shovelling the snow the rest of the time. Jasper loved it though. By the time Sunday came around I was ready to lace up the skates. I debated taking my Sinus Minus before the game, but didn't. I'd promised Lise I wouldn't. Besides I wanted to prove to myself that I didn't need it: that the whole thing was just psychological.

The guys were humming in the dressing room, and Neal was his usual lively self. Knowles gave us a great pep talk, telling us to forget about the last game and look ahead, but we didn't need it. We were fired up and it was going to take an incredible Panther team to get anything past us. I eyed Cory Martinson in the warm-up. Sometime this game, I was going to let him know what I thought of him asking Valerie to the dance.

I got my opportunity about halfway through the first period. Martinson had the puck along the boards in the neutral zone and was looking for his wingers. As soon as I saw him look around, I hit him, a crushing blow that shook the arena. The crowd screamed for a penalty, but it had been a clean check. Moments later, Justin let a long shot go from centre ice using their defenceman as a screen. The light went on. A lucky first goal, but the way we were playing, I knew it wouldn't be the last. The rink rang with the sounds of carefully executed passes and clean skating. Eight minutes later, Red managed to deflect Theo's shot over the goalie's shoulder. We were up by two at the end of the first period, and we'd held the Panthers to only three shots on net.

Knowles was elated and kept congratulating us on not letting the previous game get us down. He said we had character and guts, but I knew that we really just had Sinus Minus.

The second period started out with Neal's line generating great offense. With that kind of pressure, one of the shots or rebounds was bound to go in eventually, and go in it did. Ryan, Justin and I went on straight afterwards, determined to ride the momentum. We skated into the Panthers' end, set up the play and simply passed the puck around like it was on strings. When Martinson tried to poke-check me, I turned him inside out and skated for the net. I fed it across to Ryan who blasted it home. By the end of the second period, we were up by four and starting to talk about Geordie's first shutout of the year.

But the Panthers hadn't given up. They won the first faceoff and broke hard for the net. Their right-winger was gearing up for a slapshot when Tony sent him flying and the referee whistled him off. Neal's complaints didn't do any good, and our line went out to kill the penalty. Ryan ragged the puck from the faceoff and took it back behind Geordie. When the Panthers' wingers pressed him, he did some fancy skating, deking two forwards before shooting it end to end. James inter-cepted the goalie's pass and let a quick wrist shot go. The goalie got a piece of it, but not enough to keep it out. That short-handed goal was the final crush for the Panthers. We managed two more goals against a half-hearted squad and Geordie got his first shut-out.

I studied the faces of my teammates in the dressing room. I'd played without the Sinus Minus tonight and I'd played well. Lise was right. It was psychological. If I didn't need it, the team didn't either.

"You made a couple of nice moves on Martinson," said Ryan as we hoisted our bags to our shoulders. "Trying to tell him something?"

"Yeah!" Those checks I'd thrown had made me feel better, but they didn't erase the fact that it was Cory Martinson who was going to be holding Valerie in his arms when they played the last waltz at the Christmas dance.

CHAPTER 7

The week was a gruelling one, and having been sick the week before I'd missed a lot of the review. I spent almost all my spare time studying. All the guys were cramming and there wasn't much time for socializing. I hadn't seen Valerie since that day in the stairwell, or had much time to think about her. Math and English hadn't been too bad, but Social and French were going to be the tough ones, especially the oral French test. I was waiting for my turn when Mme Dupont sent me down to the office on an errand. I was trying to remember how to talk hockey in French when I arrived at the office and saw Valerie talking to Mrs. Ell, the secretary. She looked up at me as I gave Mrs. Ell my note. Neither of us said a word, just stood looking at the countertop until Mrs. Ell handed Valerie an envelope for one of her teachers.

She took it off the counter upside down and the contents went sprawling. I bent down to pick up the papers.

"Thanks Joel," she said.

Just hearing her say my name sent a pang through me and I felt the need to explain. "I'm sorry I didn't call you, Valerie," I began. "I was sick and studying for exams and . . . " It seemed such a lame excuse.

"I know," said Valerie. "It's wild this time of year, isn't it?"

I studied her dark green eyes as we straightened up. Was she actually glad to see me? I returned her smile and she blushed. Despite all my faults, she seemed glad to see me. "Well," I said finally, "aren't you going to tell me how you did?"

"How we did?" The colour crept higher on her cheeks.

"At the provincials," I reminded her.

"We won, Joel!"

I grabbed her hands. "You won!" I couldn't believe it. My prediction had been right. "Awesome!"

She trembled with excitement. "It was so close."

I didn't even notice the secretary trying to give me the papers for Mme Dupont until Valerie took them. She handed them to me as we left the office area.

"I told you I'd be talking to a provincial champ next time I saw you."

"You did," she said. "But it's still so hard to believe."

I wanted to put my arms around her and hug her right then, but the thought of Cory taking her to the dance stopped me. "I better get back to French," I said. "I'll see you around." I hesitated.

Her hips swayed slightly and she pressed the envelope against the curves of her body. She waited, as if contemplating something and then called after me. "Maybe I'll see you at the dance. Are you going?"

Her question caught me off guard. "Uh, I, yeah, I thought I would. Are you?"

She nodded. "Save me a dance?" she asked, looking at the floor.

I stared at her. The girl of my dreams asking me to save her a dance when she'd already agreed to go with Cory Martinson.

Talk about confusing! "Uh, sure," I agreed, "if Cory doesn't mind."

Her head snapped up. Then a look of disbelief spread across her face.

I backtracked. "I, uh, I heard that Cory asked you to the dance."

At first I didn't think she was going to answer me, just stalk off instead. "He did," she retorted. Now I was really confused. Her eyes narrowed. "And I said 'No'!"

The impact of her words hit me as she turned and marched down the hallway. I almost ran after her. But, could I ask her to go with me now, just two days before the dance? Had she been waiting for me all this time? By the time all the questions had swirled through my head, Valerie had disappeared down the corridor. I raced up the stairs to French class. I'd made a fool of myself with Valerie again, but this time I felt strangely elated. She wasn't going to be at the dance with Cory. In fact, she'd asked me to save her a dance. Then again, she'd just stamped off, obviously more than a little irritated with me. But somehow that didn't matter now. I leaped up the last few stairs. When that last waltz played, I was going to be the one holding Valerie in my arms.

I managed to get through my French test and my Social one the next afternoon. Even Ryan was breathing a sigh of relief. We bought our tickets for the dance on the way out of school.

"I'll see if Lise or Dad can drop us off and pick us up after the dance."

"Pete said his mom would give us a ride over in the van. She's taking a bunch of the other guys too. I told him you'd be at my place at seven. May as well make an entrance."

I could hardly conceal my excitement. Even Ryan seemed elated. Exams were over and he hadn't found them as bad as he'd figured he would. I could just imagine tomorrow night — walking into the gym with all the Falcons, music blaring, lights flickering. The girls would be there early of course and they'd see us come in. It wouldn't take me long to find Valerie. I chuckled silently. Wouldn't the guys be surprised when I walked over and led Valerie Sherman out onto the dance floor! Yes, tomorrow night was going to be a memorable one. I just knew it.

We spent the next day cleaning out lockers and the phys. ed. equipment rooms. The girls were decorating the gym. I didn't actually speak to Valerie, but I did smile in her direction and she did smile back.

Outside, the snow had started and the wind was whipping it into sheets by the time school finished. Lise said there was a storm warning in effect, but I hardly heard her. I wolfed down my meal and went up to change. Not that I was going to wear anything special — just my usual jeans and one of my favourite shirts, but still I needed time to make things look right. I tried parting my hair on the right, then the left, then gave up and mussed it into its usual haphazard waves. I contemplated borrowing some of Dad's aftershave, but decided against it. Lise would really be suspicious then.

It was only 6:30 when I got downstairs, but I figured I'd head over to Ryan's anyway. I hollered at Lise, took one last look in the mirror and jumped in the car. The snow was blowing straight at us making it hard to see. We crawled onto the main road and Lise took it real slow. Ryan's dad's car still wasn't in the driveway when we arrived. "Your dad will pick you up from the school," Lise hollered through the wind. I waved and dashed for the house as she drove away.

Ryan didn't answer when I knocked. Probably couldn't hear on account of the wind, I told myself. I rang the doorbell. Then, just as I was about to ring a second time, Ryan threw the door open. His eyes were wild and crazed and his shirt was half untucked. "Damn!" he cried when he saw me. "Where's the ambulance?"

I shut the door and raced upstairs behind Ryan. His mom lay listlessly on the bed, her eyes fixed on the ceiling. Her pupils were huge and dilated. Suddenly her body arched and began to shake. Ryan grasped her hands. I heard Ryan's dad come into the house about the same time as I heard the sirens in the distance.

Mr. Davis rushed to his wife. His eyes swept wildly around the room and he grabbed an empty box off the night table. "Sleeprite," he said. I stared at the familiar package of sleep medicine.

The sirens blared, then died. "I'll meet them," Ryan cried, racing down the stairs. I followed him to the landing, stepping aside as the paramedics took the steps two at a time, with Ryan in the lead. "Sleeping pills," he answered as he led the way into the bedroom and Mr. Davis held up the empty package.

I went downstairs to close the front door. The snow had already filled the doorway and white footprints dotted the carpet on the stairs. The doorbell rang again and I opened it to see a police officer standing in the light.

"You've got a medical emergency here, son?" he asked.

I pointed upstairs.

"What happened?"

"It's Ry's mom." My voice cracked and I started again. "My friend's mom tried to commit suicide." The words stuck in my throat.

"An overdose?"

I nodded numbly.

"She was home alone?"

"No, Ryan was here."

Together, we walked up the stairs. A stretcher lay on the floor beside a big, gray toolbox full of emergency equipment. Ryan and his dad hovered behind the paramedics who had already put Mrs. Davis on oxygen. I heard the velcro of a blood-pressure cuff being unstrapped. "140 over 90." An arm yanked a black box out of the kit amidst snippets of conversation. "Heart monitor . . . another seizure . . . blood sugar."

The police officer put a hand on my shoulder. "It looks like everything's under control here." He steered me towards the door. "We'll wait downstairs."

It wasn't long before the paramedics' foot-steps pounded down the stairs. Strapped flat on the stretcher was the frail body of Ryan's mom. We stepped aside and they disappeared into the storm.

Mr. Davis climbed into the ambulance with his wife. "I'll follow with the boys in my squad car," shouted the officer into the wind as the doors of the ambulance closed. "Take it easy fellows," he added.

From the front walk, Ryan and I watched the ambulance drive off. "Why don't you boys grab your coats and lock up the house?" the policeman said. "You'll probably just have to wait at the hospital anyway." We shuffled back to the doorway in silence. I found Ryan's Falcons jacket on the chair near the front door and he went to check the back door.

"Ryan, I'm sorry, I, I . . . " I faltered.

Ryan's eyes clouded over. Then abruptly, he slammed his feet into his sneakers and slipped his arms into his coat. He locked the door behind us and we fought our way through the storm to the police car.

The officer carried on a running one-sided conversation all the way to the hospital. Every once in awhile I tried to respond to his comments about the weather or the National Hockey League — he'd seen our jackets — but I only managed half-hearted answers. Ryan stared blankly out the window while the police officer prattled on. It took us a long time to reach the hospital with all the traffic and accidents. The officer told us that the ambulance would have been much faster. He dropped us at the emergency entrance and wished us luck.

I followed Ryan into the emergency room. The place was packed. Ryan made his way to the reception desk. The receptionist asked him who he was, then said that Mrs. Davis had been registered, but she didn't know how she was doing. She told us to sit and wait. We picked our way to two empty chairs.

I knew there wasn't much point in saying anything, but I felt like I had to try. "This is a good hospital, Ry. They handle stuff like this all the time." I watched the expressionless face beside me. "It'll be all right, Ryan. I have this feeling." I had no such feeling, but the words just came out. Maybe I was trying to convince myself as much as Ryan. I kept seeing Mrs. Davis lying on the bed. I'd never seen anyone look so . . . so lifeless.

I studied the other people around me. Some, like the guy opposite with his arm in a makeshift sling, were waiting for treatment, but others, like us, were waiting for news. Some of them looked like they'd been there for a long time. And every so often, we heard the sirens come up the hill.

Eventually, I stood up to stretch my legs. "I'm just going to let Dad know where I am," I told Ryan. "Want a chocolate milk or something?" There was no response.

I manoeuvred my way through the emergency room to the telephones and dropped a couple of coins in the slot. Lise answered. "Lise, it's Joel. Listen, could you tell Dad that I'm at the hospital."

"Hospital!" she shrieked. "Steve! Joel, where are you? What's happened? We'll be there in a minute. Are you hurt?"

"Lise, Lise, take it easy." By that time, Dad was on the phone. "Dad, listen, I'm fine, okay." I heard him exhale in relief.

"Lise said you were at the hospital. What's going on?"

"Ryan's mom tried to commit suicide. I guess it happened just before Lise dropped me off at Ryan's place. He'd already called the ambulance."

"Where's John?" Dad asked.

"He's here, I think. He got home just before the paramedics arrived and went in the ambulance with Mrs. Davis. A cop drove Ryan and I up."

"Are you at the Rockyview?"

"Yeah, in the emergency room. So far we haven't heard anything."

"I'll be right there, son," said Dad.

"Sure, Dad." I was about to add that he didn't really need to come, but he'd already hung up. There wasn't a whole lot anyone could do — just wait to hear how Ryan's mom was. A woman, sobbing violently, came through the doors into the waiting area. I stood staring after her. Then again, maybe it was a good idea if Dad did come. I plugged the machine and picked up the two chocolate milks. My hands were trembling. What would happen if Ryan's mom didn't make it this time? If the ambulance had been too late?

I searched for Ryan in the crowd. He was leaning over in his chair, his hands clenched, his eyes staring at the floor. I crossed the room and sat back down in my seat.

"I brought you a chocolate milk."

Ryan glanced up at me. "You okay?" he asked.

I was sure I looked pale. "Yeah," I managed, amazed that he'd noticed.

He looked around, for the first time. "It's not a great place, is it?"

I shook my head and sipped my milk.

"Look, Joel, I'm sorry about all this tonight." Ryan sighed. "I forgot. You're supposed to be at the Christmas dance."

I looked blankly at him. It was the farthest thing from my mind.

"Why don't you call your dad and see if he can pick you up?" He looked towards the desk. "I expect there will be some news soon . . . " His voice trailed off.

I found my voice. "That's okay, Ry. I'll stick around. You know, you might want . . . uh, you know." We drank our milk in silence until Dad burst through the doors.

I don't remember a time I was so glad to see him. He hurried over to us and put a hand on each of our shoulders. "How are you boys doing?"

I shrugged.

"How long have you been here?" he asked, eyeing the desk.

I studied my watch. "Maybe an hour or so."

"And you haven't had any word from your dad?" Ryan shook his head and from his eyes I knew that he, too, was glad that my dad had shown up. "Does he know you're here?"

Ryan looked confused.

"The cop told the paramedics he'd bring us up. I think Mr. Davis heard him," I said.

Dad walked over to the desk and spoke to the receptionist. "The nurse is going to let your dad know you're here," he explained. "He should be out shortly."

Within minutes, Mr. Davis strode out into the waiting room. "Ryan, I'm sorry! I didn't know you'd come up! I registered her and then went back inside. How did you get here?"

"How is she, Dad?"

Mr. Davis sighed. "It was pretty touch and go, son. They pumped her stomach and gave her charcoal, so hopefully that will absorb whatever's left in her system. She's starting to respond and things look pretty good."

I watched Ryan's body relax and tried to imagine how he must have been feeling for the last hour or so. "You can come in and see her," he said, "if you like."

"Okay," said Ryan.

Mr. Davis turned toward us. "Steve, Joel, thanks very much for coming up. I haven't been thinking clearly. The boys shouldn't have been waiting out here . . . "

"Don't worry about it, John." Dad gestured toward the corridor. "Go ahead and I hope all goes well."

We watched Ryan and his dad pass through the white doors with the tiny windows. "Let's go," said Dad gently. "You can't do anything else for Ryan tonight."

Dad was right. I followed him to the elevators and down to the underground parking. He didn't say anything. By the time he'd unlocked the car, I felt as if I could fall asleep on the spot. "You guys were going to the Christmas dance tonight, weren't you?" Dad asked. "I can still take you by the school if you like."

I closed my eyes and leaned back against the headrest. "Take me home, Dad, please."

I slept in until 9:00 the next morning. Lise hovered around me, but didn't say anything about the previous night. She dropped me off at school late. It was only a half-day to pick up our exam marks anyway. Somehow the word had got out and the guys all crowded around me at class change with a thousand questions. I didn't know where to start and I never had a chance to. Mr. Winter, our guidance counsellor, caught up with me in the hallway and asked to speak to me. I followed him back to his office.

"Mr. Davis called the school this morning to explain why Ryan wouldn't be in. He asked if you'd take Ryan's test marks with you, so I took the liberty of collecting both yours and Ryan's grades." He pushed two envelopes across the desk. "It must have been a difficult night last night."

Mr. Winter sat silently and after a bit I found myself telling him about what had happened. "Sometimes prescription drugs can be as bad or worse than street drugs," he explained. "An overdose of any over-the-counter drug can have disastrous effects, especially if the person is sensitive to it. Of course, I have no idea how Ryan's mom will be in the long run. She obviously needs help. I think you know she's been ill for some time."

I nodded.

"I expect you were a great support at the hospital last night, Joel."

"I didn't do much," I said.

"Sometimes just being there is all anyone can do." Mr. Winter paused. "It might help if Ryan could talk to you Joel, but that may not be easy for you."

I looked up.

"How are you doing, anyway?"

"Uh, fine, I think," I said.

"And the other boys — the rest of the hockey team?"

I shrugged. "I don't know. I haven't said anything to them. I don't really know what to tell them."

"If I were you, I'd give them the basics and leave it at that."

Suddenly, I could see the snowy footprints on the steps and hear Ryan filling in the paramedics as they took the stairs two at a time. I thought about how Ryan had taken control at the house, his stony silence at the hospital and then how he'd said I should go to the dance afterwards. What would I have done if I'd been in his shoes?

Mr. Winter was talking to me again. Something about Christmas being an especially tough time of year for lots of people. "It's not uncommon for people to attempt suicide during the holiday season. It seems to bring out the best and the worst in people." Mr. Winter droned on for a few more minutes then let me go.

I wandered through the empty hallways on my way to my locker and escaped from the school with the envelopes Mr. Winter had given me. Lise honked as I came through the doors and I had to admit that I was glad to see her.

"I was just passing by, so I thought I'd give you a lift," she lied.

"Thanks," I said, slamming the car door.

"What are those?" She indicated the brown envelopes.

"Exam marks, but I haven't looked."

She reached across the front seat and touched my elbow. "Did you manage okay this morning?"

"Yeah," I said. "I think so." The morning was already a blur. We rode home in silence.

After half an hour of staring blankly at the television, I mustered the courage to look at my marks. I hadn't done particularly well in French, but my marks were solid. I threw Ryan's envelope on the table in front of me and wondered how he'd done. I debated about having a look, but didn't in the end. The way things were at his house now, it wasn't likely that his dad would say too much. I hadn't even called yet today, but the telephone seemed pretty impersonal after all we'd been through last night.

"I think I'll go over to Ryan's," I called up the stairs to Lise.

She hurried to the top of the staircase. "Do you want a lift?"

I shook my head. "No thanks, I'll take Jasper for a walk."

Jasper raced in circles through the snowdrifts. The snow had stopped late last night, but the roads were still not completely cleared and the wind had left huge, white crests. Jasper crashed into these, full force, his black nose plowing out the other end, his coat covered in white flakes. We cut across the park where the community had flooded a portion of the playground to make a little kid's skating rink. It was empty, but someone had made a half-hearted attempt to clear it and Jasper hit the ice full out, his front legs sliding too far in front and his back legs pedalling like crazy to catch up. He hit the snowbank on the far side and looked back. I called him over and rubbed his ears. "Crazy mutt." We stuck to the side streets so I didn't have to put Jasper on a lead, and it was almost mid-afternoon when we reached Ryan's.

Mr. Davis' car was in the driveway. I put Jasper in the backyard and wondered what I was supposed to say. Mr. Davis answered the door, showed me in and called upstairs. Ryan came down. His hair stood almost straight on end and it was pretty obvious that he'd just woken up.

"Nice hair!"

Ryan's eyes drifted to the envelope.

"Marks," I said. "Mr. Winter asked me to give them to you."

"Did you open the envelope?"

"No!" I said, embarrassed that I'd thought of doing so.

Ryan peered into the living room where his dad was sitting reading. "Come on," he whispered.

Upstairs in his room, he took a deep breath and opened it. A slow smile spread across his face. "Swystun, you're not going to believe this." I tried to peer over his shoulder, but he pulled the paper away. "I passed them all. Even Math." I put up my hand for a high five and he gave me one. "Truth is, I didn't think I had a chance."

I took the outstretched paper and scanned the marks. They were mostly 50s with an odd 60. My father would have flipped out if I'd brought home marks like these. I looked around Ryan's room. I'd been in it hundreds of times. It could have been my own — the furniture, the hockey posters, the bed. I studied the ceiling — even the stucco was the same.

Did Ryan stare at the stucco on his ceiling? After last night, I was sure he did, and yet we never talked about stuff like that. What had Mr. Winter said? That it might be good for him to talk about it — but not so easy for me. I took a deep breath. "How's your mom?"

I could see the muscles in his neck tense up. "The doctors think she'll be okay." He paused. "Whatever that means."

I could have just said something like "That's good" and closed the topic, but this time I didn't. "Did you see her last night?"

He nodded. "She was still unconscious. We're going back up this afternoon."

He stopped and I had no idea where to go from there. There was a moment of silence. I fought the urge to change the subject.

Then suddenly he picked up where he had left off. "Even if she is conscious, she won't know us. At least she didn't last time." He sighed and I let him talk. "Every time it happens, she gets worse and worse. I don't know how much farther she can go, but she keeps trying." He looked up at me.

I managed a sympathetic smile.

"I thought she was sleeping upstairs. She does that often you know. Just goes up and lies down like she's asleep — any time of the day or night. I should have checked on her, Joel, but I was too busy wondering when Dad would make it home so I could go to that dumb Christmas dance."

"It wasn't your fault, Ry."

"And who knows how long before that she'd taken them."

"You can't be beside her night and day."

We sat silently. "The doctors keep telling us that it's a chemical imbalance. That if they can just find the right combination of drugs, they might be able to help her." His eyes stared through me. "It's not fair, Joel. Why can't she just be like other mothers?"

I let Ryan's words sink in. Other mothers? Like my mother?

Jasper barked outside and Ryan's dad hollered upstairs. It was almost time to go to the hospital. "I'd better show him these," said Ryan picking up his grades.

"And I'd better go before Jasper tears up your yard."

Mr. Davis came to the bottom of the stairs. "Thanks for coming by, Joel."

I made my way down the side streets with Jasper. For the first time ever, Ryan and I had had a real conversation. Mr. Winter was right. I think it had helped him, even though I hadn't really said anything. I broke into a jog and whistled for Jasper. Angie was supposed to be coming home tonight and Dad started his holidays next week. Suddenly, I wanted nothing more than to be home, with everyone, Angie, Dad and yes, even Lise.

CHAPTER 8

We had a couple of practices before Christmas and then a few days' break before the tournament started. Dad was off and Angie home from university with a never-ending supply of stories. She and Lise spent hours bustling about the kitchen and chatting. Dad and I went skiing, tobogganing and we all went to the wave pool. I phoned Ryan a few times, but he declined my invites. I got the feeling that he wasn't keen to leave his dad alone. Lise asked if I'd like to invite Ryan and Mr. Davis round for Christmas dinner, but I knew they'd already accepted another invitation.

Dad and I hadn't done any shopping and finally headed out on December 23rd, one day earlier than usual. I picked out a new rucksack for Angie and a wild patchwork sweatshirt for Lise. Angie and I had gone in together on a pair of binoculars for Dad. "All done?" Dad asked, staggering towards the spot where we'd agreed to meet.

"Yeah, have you ever seen so many people in your life?"

He laughed. "Did you get what you wanted for everyone?"

"I think so."

He stopped walking and looked serious for a minute. "Did you pick up a little something for Ryan?"

His question caught me off guard. Normally, Ryan and I never exchanged gifts. "No, I didn't," I said, "but I'd like to."

"We'll get something on our way out," Dad replied, ruffling my hair with a proud look in his eyes.

We stopped at the mega sports store in the mall and I bought Ryan a Penguins' cap. He collected them and I knew he didn't have that one.

The next day was Christmas Eve, the day we trimmed the tree. Dad had his own traditions. The tree couldn't be decorated before mid-afternoon so that when the lights were turned on, it would be dark outside. It had to be done while singing Christmas carols and we always picked numbers to see who put the star on top.

Lise was off to do the final grocery shop in the morning and Angie had offered to go along. Dad and I were wrapping presents while Bing Crosby belted out Christmas carols on the stereo. I had just wrapped Ryan's cap and was thinking about zipping over to see him when there was a knock on the door. Ryan stood in the doorway, a package in his hand.

"Merry Christmas, Swystun."

I took the gift as Dad came to the door behind me. "Ryan," he called, "is your dad with you?"

Ryan jerked his head towards the driveway as I went to fetch my present. Dad jammed his feet into his shoes and disappeared outside. In a few minutes, he was back with Mr. Davis. "Come on in. It's just us guys today. We were wrapping our last few gifts and thinking about having a drink. This is the perfect excuse." Mr. Davis stepped into the house. His face was hollow and drawn, his eyes sunken and he looked noticeably thinner. Dad poured a beer for each of them and put out a plate of Christmas baking. I grabbed a few Cokes for Ryan and me and we sat down in the family room. It didn't take me long to realize how talented my father was when it came to putting people at ease. In just a few minutes, Mr. Davis had relaxed and he and Dad were swapping stories. The talk soon turned to hockey and the Falcons' chances of winning the Christmas tournament.

By the time Lise and Angie got back with the groceries, both Dad and Mr. Davis had had another drink and we were all in the midst of a game of Hockey Talk, the board game my mother had sent me for Christmas last year. Lise put lunch on the table, set two extra places and called us all. Mr. Davis started to protest, but was easily persuaded to stay. I don't think he'd felt so relaxed in a long time.

But as we cleared away the dishes, I could feel reality starting to creep back in. Mr. Davis checked his watch and announced that they should probably head off to the hospital. Dad made a few general inquiries about Ryan's mom. There was no way of deceiving reality in the long run, but the afternoon had been a much-needed escape. I handed Ryan the gift I had bought him. "Merry Christmas, Ry."

We stood silently at the front window as they drove off.

That evening, after Angie had put the star on the top, we sat around the Christmas tree watching the lights blink on and off. Every so often, Lise got up to move a decoration from one spot to another. She was wearing her reindeer dress, but it didn't bother me as much this year. Besides, Rudolph's nose matched her red bangs. "It's been a great Christmas Eve," she said, sinking back onto the couch.

Dad agreed, his arm around the back of Lise's shoulders. "Yeah, it was nice having John and Ryan here this afternoon." He paused. "But it's even nicer having all of us here now."

I thought about what Dad hadn't said.

"Is Mrs. Davis going to be all right this time?" asked Angie, staring at the tree.

"I don't know for sure," I replied. "They managed to get the drug out of her system, but that's not the real problem, is it?"

Dad sat up. "No, it's not, Joel. So often there's a psychological motivation associated with drugs, even over-the-counter drugs."

"We were just studying that in Biology," said Angie.

I cringed and glanced quickly at Lise. She caught my eye but said nothing. "Mr. Winter said something like that too," I added. Lise eyed me again and I swallowed hard.

"Yes sir," said Dad stretching. "Drugs, no matter how harmless they might seem, are nothing to fool around with." He stood up. "Who wants popcorn?"

Angie jumped up and raced into the kitchen after Dad while Lise and I sat for a moment longer. "I know, I know," I whispered before she could say anything.

She moved over to sit beside me. "You know," she said, "after Christmas comes New Year's and New Year's is always a good time to make a resolution. You know, set yourself a goal, maybe with a specific time limit."

I nodded. "Okay, okay," I muttered, walking away. After all, it was Christmas and Lise didn't have to go ruining the end of this year with thoughts of the next one.

Christmas came early. Mom forgot about the time difference and called at 6:45 in the morning. She woke everyone up, so we all headed down to the tree like we'd done years ago as children. Angie loved her rucksack and admitted that she'd almost bought the identical one while she was Christmas shopping. While Dad tried out his binoculars, Lise pulled on her sweatshirt. It looked good on her. Dad and Lise had bought me a hi-tech compact stereo for my room and Angie had picked out a few of my favourite CDs. Angie dug Ryan's gift to me out from behind the tree and everyone watched as I opened it. It was a new Calgary Flames' cap; mine had gone missing from my gym locker last month. I wondered how Ryan's Christmas morning had gone.

We had brunch and then went for a walk with Jasper who couldn't figure out why everyone's pockets were full of treats. It was snowing — big, soft snowflakes that danced their way to earth — and by the time we'd returned we were all singing "I'm Dreaming of a White Christmas", which was absurd since there was at least twenty centimeters of snow on the ground already. The house smelt of turkey and salmon by the time we got back — Dad's tradition and Lise's tradition. And more food for everyone!

After dinner and pudding, we all cleaned up and then collapsed around the television. Angie was already making noises about a championship game of something or other, but I was too stuffed. Dad turned on a Christmas movie and stretched out in his recliner-rocker. I watched for a while and then excused myself to phone Ryan. In one way, I didn't want to make that phone call. I didn't want to know what I already knew — that his Christmas had been a sad, forced one. And yet, I couldn't help thinking about what Mr. Winter had said. There was no answer the first time, so I left a message thanking him for my cap.

Ryan called back just before I went to bed. "Hey Joel, where'd you ever get the idea to buy me a Penguins' cap?"

I laughed. "Same place you did, I suppose."

"Did you get some nice stuff?"

"Dad and Lise got me this incredible stereo. You've got to come over and hear it." I cranked up the volume and held the receiver up to a speaker.

"Wow! I don't even have to come over to hear it." He laughed. "What did Valerie get you?"

"Very funny," I said. "I think you can write Valerie out of my life, especially as I didn't show up at the dance." I hadn't talked to Ryan about Valerie lately and I had no desire to try to explain things to her. With all the other things happening, it didn't seem very important.

"I thought she was going to the dance with Cory."

"She turned him down." Ryan let out a long breath. "I sort of said I'd see her there, but then I didn't make it."

"Damn, Joel, you should have left — "

"Don't be an idiot!"

"Didn't you see her the last day of school?" asked Ryan.

"No," I said slowly. I didn't want to tell him about Mr. Winter's conversation with me. "But hey, she's just a girl, right?"

Ryan chuckled. "Yeah right!"

I changed the subject before he could go on. I didn't want to think about her anyway. "So, how about you. Did you get some nice stuff for Christmas?"

"Yeah, I got some nice things." He paused. "Including two tickets to a Flames' game. Dad figured maybe I could find someone to go with me."

"Awesome!"

"It's on January 12th, so don't forget."

I wasn't about to forget. I took a deep breath, wondering whether I should ask the obvious question or not. Mr. Winter's words kept ringing in my ears, and I did in the end. "Did you visit your mom today?"

At first, Ryan didn't answer and I wondered if maybe I shouldn't have said anything. "Yeah, we did," he said finally. "Dad and I went up before supper." I fought the urge to say something trivial and move on to another subject. Instead, I waited. "She didn't talk to us, but the nurses said she seemed a little better today."

"That's good news!"

"And maybe it was just my imagination, Joel, but I think she was better today." His voice was pensive. "Once when Dad was talking to her, telling her about my face when I saw the tickets, she turned her head and looked at me. She didn't smile or anything, but just for a second, her eyes didn't look so blank, you know."

I didn't know. I didn't know and I couldn't even imagine.

"Dad didn't notice anything different, but I did. It was strange."

I nodded at the other end of the phone. The whole thing was strange, but I certainly wasn't about to tell Ryan that.

"Anyway," he said, "the whole thing's strange."

Maybe we were more alike than I figured. I took a deep breath. "How was the day — you know, Christmas?"

He didn't say anything right away. "The morning was all right, I guess. I mean it was just Dad and me. We put the tree up the other day and all, but it wasn't the same. Last year Mom wasn't too bad at Christmas — you remember. And Gran and Gramps were here, so, I guess this year was a little tough because of all that . . . " His voice trailed off. "It sucked, Joel."

"Geez Ryan."

"I knew it would. When I woke up, I just stayed in bed and pretended I was asleep." He sighed. "Dad finally came in at 10:30. He tried hard, but it was bad."

I thought about our Christmas morning — the sound of paper crinkling, the exclamations of surprise and the rippling of laughter. "I'm sorry, Ryan."

"Yeah," came the honest response. "I know."

"How's your dad holding up?"

"Okay, I guess. He's got a few days off during the tournament. He can take us to some of the games."

"Great," I said. "Are you going to skate tomorrow?"

"I haven't been on the ice for four days. I think I'll forget how if I don't go soon."

I didn't think Ryan would ever forget how to skate, but I arranged to meet him at the rink at one o'clock the next day anyway. I was starting to feel a little rusty myself and our first game was on the 27th.

CHAPTER 9

The guys were pumped when they arrived at the arena on the 27th. "Our first tourney on the stuff," announced Neal. "We're going all the way!"

We were up against a team from Medicine Hat called the Hurricanes. "I don't know much about them," admitted Knowles when he arrived, "except they're a brand new team this year. I've never seen them play, so you'll just have to go out there and play good, solid hockey. Within the first few minutes, you'll know who their ringers are." He looked around the dressing room. "Play your man, all of you, and we'll know more by the end of the first period." He stood up. "You've all had a good, long break and I expect you to skate hard."

"Is this team seeded?" asked Theo.

"No," said Coach Knowles, "but don't underestimate them either."

"Are we seeded?" asked Justin.

Knowles nodded. "Number 2, right behind the Cadillacs."

The guys groaned. "Guess who we'll be meeting in the finals?"

"Never mind the finals," advised Knowles from the doorway, "we've got to get there first."

Someone banged on the door a few minutes later and we filed out in our traditional order, Geordie first and Ryan last. I was talking over my shoulder at Ryan as I reached the gate and banged smack into Justin who had stopped halfway through the gate. The whole team was sort of held up beside the gate, gawking at the Hurricanes. Ryan let out a low whistle. They were huge — taller and heavier than all of us, except maybe Red and Neal. "Where'd these guys come from?" asked Adrian.

"Another planet if they're our age," answered Pete.

"They're not so big," said Neal, trying to be optimistic. "Come on!" He skated off towards our goal where Geordie was stretching out.

Ryan gave me a little shove and we strode out onto the ice.

I glanced sideways as I skated past. They had a couple of real monsters on their team. I wasn't keen to take a check from one of those guys. I threw myself into the warm-up and tried not to worry.

"I know they're a little on the large side," acknowledged Knowles as we huddled by the bench just minutes before the whistle blew. "But size isn't everything. Just go out there and play the calibre of hockey you guys have played all season."

Justin, Ryan and I were out first. I glanced up at the Hurricanes' winger who had squared off opposite me. Reynolds, his jersey said. He must have been a full head taller than me and outweighed me by fifteen kilograms. I hunched over my stick and tried to focus. The opposing centre wasn't so much bigger than Ryan, but the two defencemen were incredibly tall and gangly. According to their jerseys, they were brothers — the

Manywounds. What a name! The whistle blew, the referee dropped the puck and the game was on.

Except our game wasn't on. Every time the Hurricanes got near us, we pulled up and gave them room to skate. Caught in the neutral zone, I watched Reynolds drive to the slot. Adrian was out front and normally he was hard to move, but today, my man just stepped around him. Geordie stopped the first shot, but Reynolds tucked the rebound in behind Geordie. 1–0 Hurricanes. Less than a minute had elapsed.

We skated dejectedly to the bench and Knowles sent out the next line. "Hey, they're not giants, just fifteen year olds," he reminded us.

Ryan plunked down on the bench beside me. "Never mind," he said, "we'll get it back."

But we struggled all period, unable to get over the mental block. The guys refused to go into the corners with them, preferring to surrender the puck. Ryan threw a few good hits, but the Hurricanes controlled the game. Knowles was frustrated and angry by the time we got to the dressing room, down by three goals. "What's with you guys? You're all running in the opposite direction every time they get near you — except for the odd exception." He glanced at Ryan. "You psyched yourselves out before you even stepped onto the ice."

We hung our heads. It was true. Only Ryan didn't seem phased by their size. Still it wasn't easy trying to overcome that mental block.

Knowles softened his tone a bit. He'd never been a screamer. "All you have to do is go out there and throw a few hard checks right off the mark. Let them know you're not afraid of them. Right now you're running like scared rabbits every time a black jersey gets close." There was a knock on the door and Justin went to see.

"Coach Knowles, it's for you," he called. "Says it's important."

Knowles went to the door and then stuck his head back inside. "I've got to go for a few minutes. Think about it, will you guys?"

The dressing room was silent for a few minutes. "Knowles is right," said Pete finally. "We have to go out there and check first thing."

"If we do that, we'll definitely have the element of surprise working in our favour," added Neal.

A few of the guys laughed. "It's either that or wave the white flag in the first game," said Carl.

"Not while we have the stuff," whispered James.

I cringed and sank back against the wall.

"Exactly," said Pete.

"That's something we've got that they don't," added Scott.

Ryan jumped to his feet. He looked like he was about to explode, but he didn't. Instead, he just stared at everyone. The room went silent. When he did speak, his voice was low and even. "The Falcons don't lie down and surrender — stuff or no stuff," he said. I watched him with interest, fighting the guilty feelings that overwhelmed me. The door opened and closed. "What difference does it make if a guy's got fifteen centimetres or ten kilos on you? Does that mean you can't outskate him? Does that mean you can't flatten him against the boards? Does that mean you can't outmanoeuvre him at centre ice?" All eyes were on Ryan, who stood in the middle of the room whispering. "How big a guy is on the ice doesn't have anything to do with his size."

"That's right," said a voice from the doorway. We looked to see Coach Knowles and another man standing beside him. It was the other man that had spoken, and he looked familiar.

Ryan sat down as Coach Knowles moved into the room. "I think you all know Phil Keefler," he said, introducing the man beside him who now stepped into the light of the room.

Phil smiled at us and a general awe of silence went through the guys. Not many of us had stood in the same room as one of the real greats.

"He's right, you know," Phil said, gesturing at Ryan. "I've skated circles around guys twice my size and sent players that towered over me to the ice with good solid checks." He grinned. "In fact, if you get down low enough, you can knock their centre of gravity out real fast."

I studied Phil Keefler. He really wasn't particularly big or heavy, although I imagined he'd probably been heavier when he was playing. Still, even now, he was solid.

He looked around at our faces. "Coach Knowles told me you guys would give us a good game at this skating showcase. I'd like to think so." He paused, rubbed his chin and pointed to Ryan. "Listen to that lad. Coach Knowles, or myself, we couldn't say it better." He winked at us, smiled and left the dressing room beside Coach Knowles.

The room buzzed. What was Phil Keefler doing here today? Were there scouts in the arena? How did he know Coach Knowles so well? The guys were still speculating when someone knocked on the door to let us know we were due on the ice.

I filed out in front of Ryan. He had that faraway look in his eyes again. And why not? Phil Keefler had just paid him a compliment, a big compliment. I nudged him in the ribs with my elbow. "You still with us?"

He grinned that trademark Davis grin that I hadn't seen for quite awhile. "You bet," he said, reaching the gate. Someone hollered his name and we looked up to see Mr. Davis, Dad and Angie sitting together. We waved. "You bet," Ryan said again, stepping onto the ice.

It was perhaps, Dad said later, the greatest transformation he had ever seen between periods. We threw seven clean, hard checks in the first two minutes and the Hurricanes must have thought they were playing a different team. By the halfway point of the second period, we'd scored twice and it was the Hurricanes that were backing off in the corners.

Our cheering section was loud in disbelief and delight. The dressing room buzzed between periods and we skated circles around them in the third period. Red got a lucky screened goal and then Theo did some fabulous stickhandling and found the five-hole. We were up by a goal, 4-3, and dominating every aspect of play. Knowles was after us to slow it down a little, save our legs for the rest of the tournament. Most of us did just that, but not Ryan. Maybe it was because he thought the scouts might be there, or maybe it was having his dad there. Whatever the reason, he was flying.

I think he could have beat the Hurricanes single-handedly in the last few minutes of play, but we went out anyway to keep him company. He nailed one more high into the corner just seconds before the end of the game and the crowd rose and applauded. I don't think he noticed though and when the buzzer went, he looked disappointed. We shook hands with a rather shaken Hurricanes team and skated off to the dressing room.

There was a lot of backslapping and self-congratulating. We'd never had such an incredible comeback before. And of course, we couldn't believe Ryan's performance. Knowles ordered us all to go home and get a good rest before tomorrow's games. Ryan said little through it all, only that he had to hurry because they were going up to the hospital to see his mom. He was one of the first to leave the dressing room, but he was still standing in the lobby with his father and Phil Keefler when I came out ten minutes later.

I caught up with him as they parted. "Phone me," I whispered in his ear.

"So what did he say?" I asked, almost clambering through the phone when he called later that night.

"Who?"

"Phil Keefler, who else?"

Ryan was trying to be nonchalant, but I could tell he was excited. "Oh, he was just talking to Dad mostly. I guess he came to the game with a couple of kids. He's one of these Big Brothers to kids who don't have fathers. They live nearby here and knew that our tourney was on, so he brought them."

"And he stayed for the whole game?"

"Yeah, it turns out that he played junior hockey with Coach Knowles. Says Knowles used to be a pretty good player in his day, but he hurt his back one season and that kind of knocked him out of the running for the big leagues. I never knew that."

I hadn't known either. Coach Knowles had never said much about his past. "Did he say anything about the team or the Old-timers' game?"

"Just that we'd made a remarkable comeback and he was looking forward to a good game in February."

"Didn't he say anything about how you played today. You were flying, Ry."

"Not really. He did say that I should have gone for the stick side on that goal I missed in the third period though."

I chuckled. "Well, I thought you had an awesome game."

"Thanks," said Ryan, "so did my dad."

I smiled. There was no doubt about it. Ryan was just a cut above the rest of us. I marvelled at his composure, his ability to take it all in stride — Christmas, his mom, everything.

At the same time, I couldn't forget the feeling of guilt that had come over me in the dressing room today. I'd given the guys an extra big batch of stuff at the last meeting — enough to get them through the tournament — but for the first time, I really wished I hadn't. What was it Dad had said about over-the-counter drugs? The limp body of Mrs. Davis flashed before my eyes. I went downstairs. Angie was sitting reading a novel in front of the Christmas tree. Dad and Lise were watching television in the other room.

"I thought you were going to bed early," said Angie.

I sat down, determined to find out what I could from her. "What's your favourite subject at university?"

She looked up in surprise. "Probably Biology, why?"

Luck was with me. "Is that where you learned about all the dangers of these over-the-counter drugs?" I asked.

She scrutinized me closely. "Mm, hmm, why?"

"Are they really that dangerous, all those pain killers and antihistamines and stuff?"

She closed her book. "Yes and no. If they're taken like they should be and you're not allergic or sensitive, then they're really no problem. But if you take too much of something, like Mrs. Davis did, then it can be a big problem."

"So it's only if you take a whole bunch at once that it's dangerous?"

"Either that or take something over an extended period. Some drugs aren't intended for continuous use."

I tried not to look anxious. "What happens if you do?"

"It depends on what type of drug it is. There can be all kinds of side effects — serious ones sometimes." She stared hard at me. "Why, Joel? Is there something wrong?"

I debated telling her the truth, but something stopped me. I guess I knew how disappointed she'd be in me. Never mind the fact that the team thought she was my supplier. "Just curious," I said, forcing a smile to my lips. "I think I'll get a snack."

She grinned. "Every time I see you, you eat more than I thought you did."

Lying in bed that night, I thought about what Lise had said about New Year's resolutions. Our win tonight and the previous one had proven to me that the effect of the stuff was all psychological. I hadn't taken it for some time now and I'd played consistently well. And I wasn't sure how much longer I could live with my guilt. Not after seeing Ryan's mom and talking to Angie. I'd just have to tell the guys my supply had dried up. I'd wean them off slowly until they realized that it was all psychological. Lise was right. I would make a New Year's resolution — one with a deadline attached — just as soon as the tournament was over.

We won our two games the next day with ease and watched as the organizers wrote "Falcons" in big felt letters in the semi-final square. The Cadillacs had had an easy time coming down from the top, but both of us faced tough teams in the next round. The Cadillacs were slated to take on the Icemen, who were always contenders, and we were up against an Edmonton team called the Hawks who'd made it to the quarter-finals last year. "Ready for the battle of the birds?" joked Neal. "We'll see who's flying that day."

We had one day off in between and I was feeling like I needed it. My legs were tired and my body bruised having taken a few too many hard checks. I spent the morning lazing around the house and then decided to take Jasper for a walk in the afternoon. The sun was shining and the snow was already melting as I headed in the direction of Ryan's house. A chinook was blowing in.

Mr. Davis and Ryan pulled up just as I arrived, but neither of them looked very happy. Jasper made a beeline for Ryan and pulled him down into a snowdrift. Normally, Ryan would have wrestled with him, but this time he just put his arms around Jasper and held him. For a moment, I wanted to turn around and leave, but I took a deep breath and joined them.

"Hi there," I said, looking from Mr. Davis to Ryan and back to Mr. Davis again.

"Hello Joel," said Mr. Davis' tired voice. Ryan was still sitting in the snow with Jasper. "We've just come from the hospital," he explained. "We had a meeting with the assessment people there." His face looked pale and aged as he turned and headed towards the house.

I glanced at Ryan who was giving Jasper a belly-rub. "Rough day?" I asked.

He jumped to his feet. "Want to take Jasper to the river?"

The river was a long way, but it was warm out and I figured Ryan needed it more than Jasper. "Sure," I said. We fell into step together, saying nothing. I waited for a while and then tried again. "How did it go at the hospital?"

But Ryan didn't answer. Instead, he bent down, moulded a snowball and threw it for Jasper. Jasper wasn't bad at fetching, but finding snowballs in the snow was a bit tricky. He raced back and forth bewildered until Ryan threw one onto a shovelled driveway. But every time he tried to pick it up, it fell apart or melted in his mouth. "Never mind, boy," I said, laughing, "you're not supposed to be able to retrieve snowballs."

Ryan gave Jasper a pat too. He seemed more relaxed and I thought about asking about the meeting with the doctors, but decided not to. He'd tell me in his own time. It wasn't until we were on our way home, having discussed hockey and more hockey that Ryan finally opened up. "We went to talk to the doctors about Mom today."

I caught my breath and waited. It was easier when you talked about things — easier in the long run, that was. "And?" I prompted.

"They're not very optimistic this time, Joel." His voice choked up. "When she's well enough physically, they want to put her in a long-term care home."

I tried to take this information in. "Until she's better?"

"Yeah, so they say. I guess there's always a slim chance that something will happen and she'll get better. It happens sometimes, for no real reason." He fired another snowball up. "But the truth is that most people don't get better once they go to those homes."

"What does your dad think?"

Ryan sighed. "He's agreed to it." He hurled another snowball high into the air. "I can't believe he's going to let them do that to Mom."

I tried to imagine what it would be like to have my mother, or even Lise, put in a home. There were times when I thought Lise belonged in one, but that wasn't the same thing.

"I guess Dad will have to pack up all her stuff and go talk to the staff at this nursing home place. They'll give her a private room if they can, but it sounds like there's a waiting list, so she'll probably have to share for awhile." He patted Jasper matter-of-factly. "I hope she doesn't end up with some real weirdo. But then again, they might think *she's* the real weirdo."

I looked hard at Ryan — an emotionless, empty Ryan — and wished like hell that I could do something to make a difference.

CHAPTER 10

Mr. Davis picked me up for our game against the Hawks the next day. He looked tired and drawn and Ryan didn't look much better. "Good luck boys," Mr. Davis said as he dropped us off. "I'd like to stay, but I think I'd better go home and sort out a few things."

I watched Ryan as we pulled our bags out of the trunk and carried them towards the entrance. Would talking about it do any good now? After all, we did have to face the Hawks in half an hour and his mind needed to be on the game. I kept my mouth shut.

Most of the guys were already in the dressing room. Knowles arrived a few minutes later and gave us the rundown on the Hawks. They had two solid forward lines, but no real ringers, so we had to watch everybody out there. They did, however, have a defenceman named Bradley who had one of the hardest point-shots in the league. According to Knowles, if we gave him time on the point, he'd blast one right through Geordie's pads. Geordie gulped and Neal made some comment about an unwanted appendectomy.

Knowles laughed. "The important thing is just to go out there and do what you did last game. One guy isn't going to win or lose a game."

I looked at Ryan. He'd certainly won games for us in the past. But I knew what Knowles was getting at. Ryan sat staring across the dressing room and I wondered if he'd heard anything Knowles had said.

"The Hawks haven't had a great year so far. They're 10 and 6 in their league in Edmonton, so I'm not anticipating that we'll have much trouble with them." He glanced around at our faces, his eyes lingering for a moment on Ryan's absent eyes. "Okay," he said finally, "let's go play some solid hockey."

We filed out and down the corridor. I looked back at Ryan as we waited for the team to squeeze through the gate and out onto the ice. "You okay?" I whispered.

"Sure," he said. "I'm fine."

But Ryan didn't seem fine. He missed three passes in the first shift and our line came off without ever posing a threat in their end. Next time out, Ryan lost the draw and then skated offside on a two-on-one break. And things didn't get any better. The Hawks' winger fed it back to Bradley who let a shot go as I moved in on him. The crowd erupted. I hadn't even seen it go by and neither had Geordie.

"Now I know what Knowles means," muttered Justin as we skated to the bench. "What a rocket!"

The guys were still talking about that shot when the period ended and we filed into the dressing room. We patted Geordie on the back. "Don't worry about it Geord," advised Adrian. "You can't stop 'em if you can't see 'em."

Knowles wasn't quite as easygoing. "You guys can't give Bradley time to set up like that. If you let them stand around in our end playing pass the puck, eventually someone's going to put it in." He paused. "And heads up! We're missing quite a few passes out there."

I glanced at Ryan who was flipping the top of the water bottle back and forth, back and forth.

The second period was no better. Justin shuffled down the bench to sit beside me as Red's line did a good job of killing a penalty. "Glad to see someone's playing decent hockey," he muttered.

I was determined to do the same. Next time out, Ryan lost the draw, but I crushed the winger into the boards. Justin managed a bouncing shot and Ryan got his stick on it, but deflected it wide. We skated off, our first decent shift of the night. I tapped Ryan's shin pads with my stick. "Nice play."

Ryan smiled up at me. "Next time," he said, and for the first time all night I had a glimmer of hope.

But my hope was shattered when Bradley blasted the puck from the blue line and made it 2-0. Then, minutes later, with time running out, the Hawks got a two-on-one break. I closed my eyes as they stormed down on Alex. The first shot hit the crossbar and bounced out into the slot. The second one went in just as the buzzer sounded. We rose to our feet, but the light hadn't gone on. The buzzer had sounded first! No goal!

"That last one was a little close," murmured Jared as we funnelled into the dressing room.

Knowles thought so too. "We're never going to score if we don't get some shots on goal. We've got to play heads-up hockey, hit those passes and fire when we have the chance."

"What's happened to our firepower?" asked Theo.

A couple of the guys looked at Ryan who was looking at his skates.

"Bradley sure has firepower," said Scott.

"Like I said before," interjected Knowles, "one player doesn't win or lose a game." Ryan tilted his chin to watch the coach. "You guys have been content to play the Hawks' game for two periods now. How about playing our game for a while? A hard-hitting, fast-skating game like we usually play." He stopped and waited.

"This is it guys," said Neal. "The last period and if we lose this one, we're out."

"That's not going to happen," growled Dave. We sat silently. I knew the guys were thinking about the stuff they'd taken the night before."

"Dave's right," said Red. "We just need three goals to put them away. We've done that before."

We looked expectantly at Ryan. Three goals in a period against the Hawks was a big order. Ryan was studying his skates again. I wanted to grab him and shake him. "And we'll do it again!" My voice surprised everyone, including me. Ryan's head snapped up. "Every one of us has a decent shot, so let's use it!" I grabbed my stick. "There's sixteen guys on this team, not one." I could feel Ryan's eyes on my back, but I didn't care. "I'm going out there to hit and shoot. Anybody else coming?"

To my surprise, Ryan jumped up beside me. "Count me in," he said, his eyes ablaze. "Anybody else?"

The team jumped to their feet in unison. The Zamboni was still on when we filed out, and when our line skated on, I knew that Ryan wasn't about to lose this faceoff. He didn't, and within seconds Justin was carrying the puck into the Hawks' end. He let a weak shot go, but at least it was a shot.

We threw ourselves into the Hawks every chance we got, and pretty soon they stopped coming at us so hard. That gave us more time to set up, and five minutes into the period I laid a pass onto Justin's stick in the slot. He gave a quick wrist shot and the light went on. 2-1 Hawks. Knowles almost leaped over the boards.

Neal's line went out next and threw some pretty scary checks. Pete got two shots on goal and their goalie had to scramble to grab the second rebound as Dave screamed down on him.

But the Hawks weren't about to lie down and die. Their coach called a time out and they came back checking hard. The rink echoed with thumps and bumps. We managed four more shots on goal before we got a lucky break. Red's shot hit the goal post, went off the goalie's arm and dribbled in. It was 2-2 with only seven minutes left to play.

"We don't really want to play an overtime period if we don't have to," said Knowles. "We need to save our legs for tomorrow. One more, guys, that's all we need."

We guzzled fluids. "One more," said Justin, elbowing Ryan.

"Give me the chance," Ryan pleaded, as he skated over to take the faceoff.

And we did just that. Thirty seconds later, Ryan lit up the light with a shot high on the goalie's stick side. It was 3-2 Falcons.

"Keep it clean, but don't stop checking," ordered Knowles. Ryan tried to hit their centre, but he spun off the check and Ryan smashed into the boards. I saw him drop his stick, but didn't think much of it until I looked around and saw Dave at centre ice. I changed up. Knowles was talking to Ryan when I reached the bench.

"What happened?" I panted.

"Probably bruised a rib," he muttered.

There were two and a half minutes left in the game and the Hawks were desperate. Bradley was teed up at the blue line, banging his stick for the puck. The winger slung it back to him, but Neal jostled him around and he couldn't get his shot away.

We changed up with less than a minute left. I jumped over the boards and Ryan followed. Except he didn't follow; he collapsed back onto the bench. Knowles hollered at Red and motioned Ryan to stay put. It was fast and furious and Geordie had to make a good save, but when it was all done, we were up by one. We skated wearily to the dressing room.

"That was quite the pep talk," Ryan noted as we made our way to the lobby.

I shrugged.

"I was pretty flat in the first two periods," he said.

"I noticed," I retorted, then softened my tone. "I figured there was some bad news about your mom."

"We saw the home this afternoon, right before the game." He paused. "If I ever get to that point, Joel, take me out and shoot me."

There wasn't time to say much more about it. Dad was waiting for us in the lobby. "You looked good out there, boys."

I glanced at him. "When did you get here?"

He grinned sheepishly. "About ten minutes ago. Why?"

Ryan and I exchanged knowing looks. "Let's just say that you wouldn't have said that if you'd been here two periods ago."

Dad raised his eyebrows. "Never mind," he said, "you got the win."

I threw my bag over my shoulder. Ryan picked up his, but it crashed back to the floor again. He rubbed his lower chest.

"I'll get that for you, Ryan," offered Dad. "I saw you take a hard check late in the period. Your ribs hurting?"

"A little," said Ryan. He let Dad carry the bag.

Dad kept up a running questionnaire about the game all the way home. We filled him in, but as we drove closer to Ryan's place, Ryan grew quiet and that absent look settled back into his eyes.

"Want to come over tomorrow afternoon and watch a video?" I asked as we pulled into the driveway. "Angie rented a couple dozen or so and we don't play until 3:30."

Ryan stared blankly at me. He hadn't heard a word. "Thanks, Mr. Swystun," he murmured.

"No problem, Ryan," Dad said. "And make sure you mention your ribs to your dad."

The door slammed and Ryan trudged toward the house. I wondered what bad news awaited him inside. "Everything okay with Ryan these days?" asked Dad as we pulled back onto the main road. "I mean, as okay as can be, considering."

I contemplated Dad's question. "The doctors think Mrs. Davis will have to go into one of those homes this time." My voice was a whisper.

Dad studied me in the rear-view mirror. "I'm not surprised, Joel," he said. "This has been going on for quite a while now and she's not getting any better. It just gets harder and harder to keep her at home."

"Ryan and his dad went to see the home before the game. I guess it was pretty tough." I furrowed my brow. I'd never been in one of those homes.

"They're not so bad, Joel," advised Dad. "They try to do lots of things for the patients. Mrs. Davis will get good care. She might even get to go out on bus tours and such. It's really the best thing for her at this stage."

"I guess so," I sighed. "But I don't think Ryan thinks so." I was still mulling this over when we got home.

"Hi Joel, did you win?" asked Lise.

I bit into an apple. "Barely."

Lise plugged in the kettle and leaned against the counter waiting for it to boil. She looked incredibly tired. Even the mood stones on her shirt were dark and muted.

"Tough day?"

She stretched. "Yeah, I've been trying to e-mail the Reviveets people all day, but I can't seem to get through. And they're not answering their phones either."

"Maybe they've turned off their batteries for good."

Lise groaned. "I don't even want to think about that possibility, thanks. Do you know how much stock I have downstairs?"

I pictured the stacks of shoeboxes in the basement. Still, Lise should have known better. The kettle whistled and she dug out a tea bag.

"You think I'm crazy, don't you, Joel?"

I stared at her back. "Sometimes," I admitted, but she certainly wasn't as bad off as Mrs. Davis.

She sighed. "Maybe you're right."

"Lise, have you ever been inside one of those nursing homes?"

Lise looked up at me in surprise. "As a patient, you mean?"

I smirked. Maybe she knew me better than I thought. "No, no, just as a spectator."

Lise sipped her tea. "It's not exactly a spectator sport, but if you mean as a visitor, yes, many times."

"Many times?"

"I used to volunteer at one years ago. Why?"

"I don't know. I've never been in one of them."

Lise settled herself into a chair. "They're not so bad, Joel. The rooms are painted with bright colours and there are lounges with televisions on every floor. Often there's a solarium or garden to sit in and the staff organizes activities and outings. It's the best place for a lot of those patients."

"What are the patients like?"

"It really varies. Some of them are there just for physical reasons — bad hearts, breathing problems, that sort of thing. Often they're quite lucid and like to visit with each other. Others have mental or emotional problems. That's not always pleasant. Their behaviour can be a little radical sometimes. I think that's tough on anybody, but the nursing staff are all well-trained and can handle it." She looked at me. "Is Mrs. Davis going in?"

I nodded.

"It won't be easy, Joel, but it's probably for the best."

That was what Dad had said too. Everyone seemed to think so, everyone except Ryan.

CHAPTER 11

I didn't see Ryan until the game against the Cadillacs the next afternoon. Last time we'd met the Cadillacs, Ryan and Dan Keller, their leading scorer, had both been out. The game had ended in a tie, but this was no mere league game. This was for the tournament championship and there could be no tie this time. The tension was thick in the dressing room. Knowles didn't have to psyche us up for this one. Instead he launched right into his pre-game strategy, reminding us that the Cadillacs had the strongest power play in the league. I studied Ryan. He was quiet but focused and I didn't think we'd have a repeat of last game. At least I hoped not. We needed him tonight.

"Falcons rule, Cadillacs drool," chanted Justin as we made the final adjustments to our equipment and headed out the door.

"Especially since we've got the stuff," murmured Pete. The guys nodded in agreement and I tried to push the nagging dilemma from my mind. Tomorrow I would worry about that. Tomorrow was New Year's Day. Tonight I needed to focus on the game.

The Cadillacs were already on the ice warming up. We skated out, took a couple of laps and let a few shots go on Geordie. He looked good — agile, quick and on top of his game.

Dan Keller squared off against Ryan for the game-opening faceoff, and Ryan won the draw. My heart soared. Tonight we were going to smoke the Cadillacs — of that I was certain.

And it certainly seemed like we would in the first few minutes. Ryan got two shots on goal and Justin got one on our first shift, but nothing went in. The Cadillacs found their rhythm and got going by the mid-period mark. The play went end to end for most of the period until O'Neill turned on the speed and got by James. Pete stepped into him as he drove for the slot and both of them went down, Pete's stick waving in the air. Pete got two minutes for high-sticking and our line went out to kill the penalty. But not for long. Smithers snagged the puck and let a shot go. It found its mark. 1-0 Cadillacs.

Justin and I skated towards the bench, but Ryan circled mid-rink, watching Knowles. Justin and I were already at the gate when Knowles ordered us back out. I glanced at Ryan as he lined up opposite their centre and felt a sudden surge of adrenaline. Ryan won the draw and sent it to Justin, who passed it across to me. As soon as it hit my stick I sent it back to Ryan, who tapped it back to Justin in the slot and boom. The light went on. We finished the period tied, 1-1.

"Nice goal, guys," congratulated Knowles between periods. "Looked like ping pong out there. Keep the puck moving and take advantage of any opportunities they give us. They're likely to come out checking hard. Hit them back but don't get drawn into taking a penalty. This team is too strong to give them chances on their power plays."

Knowles was right. I took a hard hit from Renegade, their big defenceman, who uttered a few ugly threats at the same time. They were out to intimidate us. Knowles sent our big guys out to mix it up with them. Neal dropped Robertson with an open-ice check that brought the crowd to its feet. If they wanted to play tough, we would play tough, too.

"Don't forget about the puck," Knowles urged.

Ryan and Keller stared each other down in the faceoff circle, each trying to outmanoeuvre the other. Finally, the linesman threw them both out and waved Smithers and me in. I won the draw and sent it over to Ryan who wheeled down the rink. Robertson smashed him into the boards, but he managed to freeze the puck.

"Nice work," I shouted, moving within earrange. Ryan was still leaning against the boards, clutching his ribs. I caught the look of pain in his eyes. "Your ribs?"

Together we skated to the bench with only two minutes left. It was clear that Ryan was hurting and Knowles had noticed. He let the other two lines finish off the period and grabbed Ryan as we filed out. "How are you doing there, Davis?"

I looked back over my shoulder. Ryan tried to straighten up, but even that made him gasp.

Knowles studied his face. "That doesn't look very good, Ryan. Maybe you should sit out for a while."

Ryan snapped his head up, but again the pain overcame him. "I'm sure it's just a bruise," he managed, but Knowles wasn't buying it.

"There's no point playing hurt. You might put yourself out for the rest of the season."

I hung back and waited for Ryan and Knowles to catch up. "But it's the Cadillacs and we're tied," Ryan pleaded.

For a moment, Knowles wavered. Then his eyes scanned the crowd. "I'll tell you what. Dr. Northcott's here — Jared's dad. You let him check you out and if he gives you the go-ahead, you can play."

Ryan and I waited in the corridor while Knowles went to find Jared's dad. I gave him a wistful smile as he joined Dr. Northcott in the first aid room, then pushed my way into the dressing room.

"Where's Ryan?" asked Dave.

"He's coming," I murmured, trying not to sound suspicious. The last thing we needed now was to lose our top scorer. I retied my skate and waited for Knowles to come in and give us the news.

"Good hockey, boys," said Knowles when he joined us. "You're doing everything right. Keep checking, shooting, stickhandling and play like you all can." He paused and I braced myself. "Remember, hockey is a team sport and we only win if all of you do your jobs." He looked around the room. "Now, unfortunately, we're going to have to play this period without Davis."

A chorus of questions went up.

"Dr. Northcott thinks he might have bruised or separated his ribs."

The guys groaned.

"Ryan would like to play this last period, believe me, but I'm not putting him back on. We don't want to lose him or anyone else to an injury." We sat silently. "All that means is that you guys are going to have to pick up the slack. We'll be mixing up the forward lines a bit and changing on the fly. Defencemen, you're going to have to cover on those changes. The Cadillacs will play hard right to the end. They always do."

"And so do we." It was Ryan's voice. He was standing just inside the door, his sweater off, his helmet in his hands.

I wished I had Ryan's confidence. Knowles sent Justin, Red and I out against Keller's line. I saw Keller scan the bench. "Lost Davis, have you?" Keller taunted Red across the faceoff circle. "What'd he do, break a nail?"

I pounded my stick on the ice. Red's pass hit Justin at the blue line and he sailed into the Cadillac's zone, sending a rink-wide pass across to me. I took the slapshot. The defenceman got a piece of it and Horvath made a lucky save.

But luck was not with us. Pete took two minutes for roughing on a retaliation and the Cadillacs didn't waste any time. They applied the pressure and fifteen seconds into the penalty Smithers slipped one through Geordie's legs. 2-1 Cadillacs.

Knowles called a time out and tried to rally the troops, but the guys' confidence was waning. We were down a goal, without Ryan, with twelve minutes left to play against a team who had the momentum. I tried to force those thoughts from my head and concentrate on my stickhandling, but I lost the puck in the neutral zone and the Cadillacs stormed down on Geordie again. Theo poke-checked Keller and they didn't get a shot on goal, but the play was mostly in our end and it stayed there. We were having trouble clearing the puck and Geordie was feeling the pressure. There was a lot of jostling in front of the net and finally a whistle.

This time luck was on our side. Renegade was going off for cross-checking. I glanced at the clock as Alex, James, Dave, Justin and I went out on the power play. We carried the puck in three times, but couldn't push past the defence. Red's line managed one decent shot, but Horvath made a glove save. The Cadillacs iced the puck every chance they got and by the time Dave's line went out, the penalty had expired.

The crowd roared and a deflated Falcons' line returned to the bench. We tried after that, we really did, but it was like the air had gone out of us. The Cadillacs just sat back and protected their one goal lead until the buzzer sounded. We shook hands with a jubilant Cadillac team and made our way to the dressing room. Nobody said much. There wasn't much to say.

Even Angie didn't say anything when I joined them in the lobby. I looked around for Ryan. "John took Ryan up to emergency to get checked out," explained Dad, reading my thoughts. "You can give him a call when you get home."

And tell him we lost, I thought as I climbed the stairs to my room — our second loss of the season. Nobody answered the phone at Ryan's house, so I hung up and headed to the kitchen for a snack. Lise was stirring some khaki brown mixture in a bowl. I grabbed a banana and reached for the milk.

"I'm sorry you lost today," Lise began, "but it might not be all bad."

"What's good about it?"

"Well the guys took their Sinus Minus last night, right?" she whispered.

I nodded.

"And you lost. So maybe they won't be so sold on the stuff now."

Lise did have a point. Maybe now was a good time to wean the guys off the stuff.

"Tomorrow's New Year's. It's a good time for resolutions."

"Are you making any?" I asked cheekily, eyeing her multi-media shirt with its bits of clay, paper and plastic.

"Actually, I'm making two." She scraped the mixture into a pan. "I'm going to give up home marketing."

I gagged on my milk. "But I thought you lived for retail therapy?"

She opened the oven door and ignored my remark. "It's just like you said, Joel. They're all crazes and fads anyway and I never make any money off them."

I felt a tinge of guilt. "Well, at least they give you something to do."

Lise set the timer on the oven. "I'll just have to find something else to do. Something useful."

"What's your second resolution?" I asked.

"To be a better mother."

I must have looked shocked, because she immediately turned bright red.

"Maybe mother's the wrong word," she backtracked. "I just mean a better role model, you know."

I said nothing. Mother was definitely the wrong word! I was still reeling when I got to my room.

Dad poked his head in a few minutes later. "Lise told me about your conversation," he began. I looked away. "Her intentions are good, Joel. She just wants you to respect her." Dad waved his hands awkwardly. "Try and be patient. Those are difficult resolutions for Lise and I admire her for making them." He closed my door behind him.

Maybe Dad was right. Those were tough resolutions for Lise. If she could make those kinds of resolutions, then I could too. I had some heavy thinking to do, and I'd start as soon as I gave Ryan the bad news.

"That's too bad," groaned Ryan when I told him. "I wish I could have been there."

"Yeah. What did they say at the hospital anyway?"

"Separated ribs. The doctor says I'll need at least a month."

"A month! Just our luck."

"Your luck. What about mine?" asked Ryan. "First we lose the tournament and then I get sidelined for a month."

"I know Ry. It's just that it's going to be hard slugging without you."

"The guy at the hospital said I'll probably be able to skate in a couple of weeks, but I can't take any physical contact for a month."

"At least you'll be able to practise before Denver."

"Yeah."

I could hear Mr. Davis hollering at Ryan.

"I've got to go Joel, we're going up to the hospital to see Mom."

"How's she doing anyway?" I asked.

"About the same. We're moving her into the home next week."

I didn't say anything. What was there to say?

CHAPTER 12

Dad and Lise had a few friends over for New Year's Eve. It didn't get too crazy or anything, but I slept in until 11:20 the next morning. The tournament had taken its toll on me. My body creaked and complained and I had a couple of good bruises. I chose a comedy from the stack of videos on the coffee table and was just getting to the hilarious part when Lise joined me on the couch.

"So, have you given any thought to your resolution?" she asked.

"You're so subtle," I told her.

"You promised, Joel. And you really need to do something soon, or this whole thing's going to go bad."

"It already has." I turned up the volume.

Lise rubbed her palms together. "We have to talk, Joel. We need to come up with a concrete plan and a deadline."

"Do we have to do it now, in the best part of the movie?"

She sighed and got to her feet. "No, but it has to be soon."

There was a note of authority in her voice that I couldn't recall ever hearing before and it really riled me. "Is this part of your New Year's resolution?" I challenged.

Lise looked back over her shoulder. "You asked me to help. That's all I'm trying to do." She paused. "And I'm feeling pretty . . . responsible."

I stared at the television.

"I guess I should be," she continued. "It's gone on too long."

"Don't you think I know that?" I shot back at her as she left the room.

I continued to stare at the television, but I couldn't hear anything the actors were saying. As much as I hated to admit it, Lise was right. Something had to be done. I turned the video off, stole the calendar off the wall in the kitchen and loped upstairs.

Today was January 1st. Easter was March 14th this year and our regular season play would be finished by then. The Denver tournament was during Easter and the Old-timers' game was the last weekend in February. Playoffs would start shortly after Easter. I tried to figure in all the variables.

We'd just lost our second game of the year, our first game on the stuff. I could just do as Lise suggested and try to convince the guys that the stuff wasn't working anymore. Maybe I could even come up with some lame medical stats about prolonged use and a decline in performance. If we lost a few games, we'd still make the playoffs, although we couldn't lose too many. Then again, if we started losing, that just might blow our confidence completely. And now Ryan was going to be out for a month. That alone would undermine the guys' confidence. I studied the calendar. Ryan would be out until the end of January. And when he came back, he'd come back flying. Maybe that was the time to wean the guys. There would still be a month left before the Old-timers' game. It would be nice to be clean for that one and then we wouldn't have to worry about Denver or playoffs in March.

I leaned back in my chair and tried to think through the particulars. As far as not having the stuff, I'd just have to tell them my supply was drying up. We could afford to lose a few games and if things got really bleak, I could always manage an odd dose of Sinus Minus for a few of the tougher games. I circled February 14th. But by Valentine's Day, it had to be all over. Finished! Done! History! They'd get over it. They'd have to. And I'd finally be able to stop staring at the ceiling.

"It'll be all over by Valentine's Day," I said aloud. There, I'd made my resolution. I felt strangely elated and nervous. What if it didn't go according to plan? It had to. I was in control and I'd make it work.

But my hand trembled as I pinned the calendar back up in the kitchen. Lise had her head buried in a magazine at the kitchen table. She looked up as I jammed the thumbtack into the wall. "You're a month ahead," she said. I looked at the calendar that still showed February. "And why is the 14th circled? Something special going on for Valentine's?"

"It's a deadline."

Lise raised her eyebrows. "Great. You'll have to tell me all about it."

"Later," I said as Angie sailed into the kitchen.

"Sounds good," said Lise when I'd told her my plan the next day. "But are you sure you can't do it earlier? I'd rather not have all those boys on Sinus Minus for another whole month."

I shook my head. "Nope. It all hinges on Ryan's return. And he won't be back until the end of January."

Lise sighed. "Okay," she said. "But that's a deadline you have to keep."

"I will."

"Now, before you go, I want to run a few thoughts past you." She dug out some notes. "I've had a few meetings with the skating showcase organizing committee and we've come up with some pretty good ideas."

I looked suspiciously at her notes. "No Hollywood on Ice, I hope."

"No, but we did think it would be good if all the performers could get together. After all, you'll all be skating on the same ice surface and it would be kind of fun if you knew each other."

I wondered if Valerie would even acknowledge my existence. I hadn't bothered to contact her over the holidays. She was bound to be ticked off at me for not showing up at the dance, and besides, Theo had run into her in the mall with some guy he hadn't recognized. Probably a new boyfriend. "What did you have in mind?" I asked Lise.

"Oh, I don't know. Just something simple off the ice — maybe involving the synchronized skaters and the Falcons. Do you think the guys would go for that?"

"Probably, depending on what it was."

Lise doodled on her notes. "Nothing's definite of course, but we were wondering about an old-fashioned lunchbox social. You know, where the girls make a lunch and then the boys bid for them without knowing whose they are." I stared at her. "Then the two of you go off for a picnic somewhere." She stopped scribbling and looked desperately in my direction.

"A picnic — in February?"

"Well, we could bring blankets and do it in a hall somewhere . . . "

"And dress up in old-fashioned suits and top hats, while the girls wear those big hoopy dress things and carry umbrellas."

Lise looked surprised. "Well yes, I suppose we . . . "

I pushed my chair back and tried to envision Red in a three-piece suit. "You," I said, laughing, "are crazier than I ever imagined."

"I said it wasn't definite," Lise protested. She wrung her hands together. "Look, all we're trying to do is get the two biggest groups to mix a little."

I pushed my chair back. "Absolutely not!"

"Come on, Joel," pleaded Lise. "Do me a favour and just run the idea of meeting up with the synchronized skaters by the guys at your next meeting, okay?" I hesitated. "So, what do you say? Just mention it and see what kind of feedback you get?"

"The idea of getting together?"

"Yeah."

"All right," I agreed. "I can do that, but no more weird stuff." I left her staring dejectedly at her papers.

Ryan bowed out of the next weekly meeting. "Dad and I are taking Mom over to the home. I don't think I'll really feel like coming. Besides, I won't be playing anyway."

"Sure," I said. "Have you told any of the guys how long you'll be out?"

"A couple of them know I have a rib injury, but I haven't told any of them it'll be a month." He paused. "Except you."

"You figure it's better to let them know game by game?"

Ryan shrugged. "Who knows? I might even be back earlier than they figure."

He went off to meet his dad and I headed for the bus stop feeling quite pleased with myself. At least I was still encouraging him to talk. And Ryan's game-to-game strategy was a good one. It would keep the guys going until he was back in action and if I knew Ryan, he wouldn't be out a month.

I was still in a good mood when the waitress brought the pizza at the meeting. I'd just given everybody their stuff for the week and I was ravenous. "Oh, by the way," I said, licking tomato sauce off my fingers, "Lise is involved in planning this skating showcase weekend and she wants to know if we'd like to get to know the synchronized skating team."

The guys hooted. "Did she say how well we should get to know them?" snickered Scott.

"I expect we should get to know all of them," added Jared.

"Is that all of them or each of them, or all of each of them?"

We laughed. Losing to the Cadillacs hadn't been easy, but it was a brand new year and anything could happen in a new year. "It should be an awesome weekend," I said.

"I'll say. I'm not sure what the highlight will be. Playing with the Old-timers or playing with the girls," said Neal.

"Will Ryan be back by then?" asked Carl suddenly.

"Of course. It's not until February," said Pete. "How long's he gone for anyway?"

"I don't think they really know." I smiled. "But this is Ryan we're talking about. How long do you think they'll be able to keep him on the sideline?"

The guys chuckled and slurped their drinks. "I thought ribs took a long time to heal," noted Jared, but I quickly changed the subject.

By the time I got home, I was pretty optimistic. If all went well, sometime in the next month the team would be off Sinus Minus. I was just settling into my homework when Ryan called.

"Joel, it's me."

"Hey, Ry, how's it going?"

At first there was no response. Then I heard him take a few deep breaths.

"Everything okay, Ry?" My mind raced and I remembered that they'd taken his mom to the home tonight. "How did it go at the home?"

Ryan's voice seethed with anger. "They tied her down, Joel!"

"Tied her down?"

"In some kind of straitjacket thing. Two nurses held her and tied her down."

"But why, what happened?"

There was silence again. I waited and Ryan finally started to talk. "We picked her up from the hospital after school, you know. Then we decided to take her out for an early supper.

She hardly ate anything, but it was fine. She just sat there like she always does and the waiter was pretty good about it all. Turns out his grandmother has the same sort of thing. Anyway, we had all her things with us in the car, so after that we just drove to the home. Dad was talking to her all the way there. Of course, she never said anything, but he explained it all anyway, so she'd know."

He paused. "The head nurse showed us to Mom's room. It wasn't as bad as I thought it was going to be. The walls are kind of a light purple and there's a flowery bedspread. She's got her own night table and dresser. She has to share a bathroom with the other lady in the room, but there's a big curtain that divides the room. It was okay."

I murmured and Ryan continued. "We sat Mom down on a chair and unpacked her things. Most of her clothes had to go to the laundry to be labelled, but we put up some pictures and a few knick-knacks she's always liked. Mom just kind of sat there staring around. Then they brought us a wheelchair for her. She can still walk, but they said it would be easier to show her around. The nurse was pretty decent. And she didn't talk like Mom wasn't there, if you know what I mean."

I didn't, but I just kept on listening.

"So we moved her into the chair and the nurse took us on a tour. I've seen it before, but Mom hasn't. We saw the lounges and the dining room and all the wings. Lots of the patients were coming out of the dining room by the time we got back. Some of those people are real loony tunes, Joel." He exhaled. "When we got back to Mom's room, her roommate was there. She's this huge, fat woman with all these health problems and she never shuts up, but at least she's still got her wits about her. Like the nurse joked, she'll eat and talk enough for her and Mom."

"That's . . . that's good," I managed.

"So anyway, after a while, we figured we'd better go. The nurse offered to bring Mom down to the lobby to say good-bye, but Dad thought it might be better if she stayed in her room with her things. He didn't figure she'd know we'd left anyway." Ryan took a deep breath. "Well, we got about halfway down the hall, and she started screaming, screaming her lungs out. She just kept screaming 'No, no, no!' Then the next thing we know she's trying to run down the hall towards us. We went back of course, but we couldn't calm her down. Every time we got near her, she hit us with her fists. Finally, these nurses came and put her in a straitjacket. Then they called the doctor to get some drug to calm her down. She was still screaming when we left."

I let Ryan's words sink in. "What are you going to do?"

"Dad's going back tomorrow morning to see if she's any better." He sounded incredibly tired. "I just don't know how he can leave her there."

I recalled Dad's and Lise's words. "Maybe things will be better in the morning," I suggested hopefully. "After she's had a good rest."

Ryan sounded skeptical. "Yeah, maybe."

CHAPTER 13

B ut things were no better when Mr. Winter paged Ryan out of phys. ed. He was gone by lunch. I stopped by Mr. Winter's office on my way to the cafeteria. "Ryan's dad called the school. Something about a meeting with the doctor." I nodded mutely. "Ryan's going to need you more than ever in the next little while, Joel."

I tried Ryan's home number after school, but nobody answered. Lise dropped me off at the rink at 5:30. "Good luck," she called. "Break a leg."

I raised my eyebrows at her. Hockey was not her strong point.

But it was ours that night. We weren't spectacular, but we didn't have to be. We just played a good, solid game and ended up with a 2-1 win over the Patriots. Knowles was delighted that we hadn't let Ryan's absence put us off our game, but I knew the guys credited the stuff with the win. I had been right in not weaning them off now. Once Ryan was back, it would be another story.

Ryan was home when I telephoned. "We won," I told him.

"Me too!" he exclaimed.

"What?"

"Dad's finally agreed." I waited silently. "He's asked the doctors to take her out of the home."

I wasn't sure if that was good or bad. "When did he change his mind?"

"After the nurses told him she woke up screaming and flailing this morning."

"Wow!"

"She didn't want to be there. She didn't want to be in that place."

"No?"

"No! That's why she screamed so much. I'm sure of it." He rushed on. "That shows she stills knows what's going on, Joel. She still has some willpower, deep down inside her. If they can just find it somehow."

For the first time in years, Ryan was seeing a glimmer of hope. "They will," I said, suddenly catching his optimism.

But finding it wasn't going to be easy. They moved Mrs. Davis back to the hospital, but the first week was a disaster with the doctors fiddling with medication and diet. Mr. Davis almost threw in the towel right then and there, but Ryan talked him out of it. I'd rarely seen Ryan so determined, except on the ice of course.

We won our game on the weekend and Knowles announced that he'd managed to get some early morning ice twice a week at an arena just down the road from the school. He wasn't going to make it official practice time because he couldn't be there himself, but if we wanted to show up and skate before classes, it would definitely help our training for Denver. I passed on the information to Ryan and he reminded me of the NHL game tickets for the 12th.

I didn't make it to any early morning skates that week, but I did get to the NHL game with Ryan. And it was a great one. The score was tied after two periods when we headed out to the kiosks for some more popcorn.

"Ryan?" asked a voice at our side.

I turned to find myself staring at Phil Keefler. "Mr. Keefler, hello," managed Ryan, juggling his popcorn.

"You boys enjoying the game?"

"It's great!" Ryan indicated me over his shoulder. "This is Joel Swystun. He plays on my line."

I said a quick hello.

"Where are you sitting?" Phil asked.

"Section 226, in the nosebleed section, but at least we're here."

Somebody bumped us from behind and we stepped aside. "If you like, you can join me in our box. We've got a couple of spare seats up there."

I caught Ryan's eye. "Cool!" we chorused and followed Phil back to his box seats.

I don't know if it was sitting in a box seat with Phil Keefler, but the game really picked up in the third period and we were all screaming and hollering right through the overtime which ended in a 3-3 tie.

"I think they ought to go to penalty shots like they do in the Olympics," I said as we manoeuvred through the crowd.

We were almost down on the ground level. "Do you boys have a ride home?" asked Phil.

"Dad will pick us up at the train station," said Ryan.

Phil pulled on his coat. "You live in the southwest, don't you?" We nodded. "So do I. Give your dad a quick call and tell him I'll drop you off."

Phil Keefler was one decent guy. I was totally convinced by the time he'd dropped me at my house and continued on to Ryan's.

The team turned green with envy when Ryan and I filled them in about the NHL game at lunch the next day. "And that's not all," whispered Ryan to me after I'd done my best to impress them with every detail about Phil Keefler that I could remember. "Dad invited him in for a drink when he dropped me off and he stayed. Naturally, I had to go to bed, but I heard the door around 11:30, so he must have stayed until then."

"What did they talk about?"

"I couldn't hear much. Something about helping out — sort of like an assistant coach, I think."

"Really?" I could hardly wrap my head around having Phil Keefler as a coach.

Ryan shrugged. "I'm not sure and Dad wouldn't say much this morning."

"Figures."

"I quizzed him all the way to the doctor's office, but I couldn't get anything out of him."

"Oh yeah, what did the doctor say about your ribs?"

"I can start skating anytime. Want to come tomorrow before school?"

I winced. That meant giving up an hour and a half's sleep, but I hadn't actually made it to any of the morning skates yet. "Sure," I muttered. "I'll see if Dad will drop us on his way to work."

We were the only two there the next morning. Ryan was ecstatic to have the blades back on and even I had to admit that there was something peaceful about an almost-empty hockey rink early in the morning. We were in high spirits as we traipsed down the road to school, our skates slung over our shoulders.

"So, have you run into Valerie lately?" asked Ryan, kicking a snowball onto the road.

I shook my head. I hadn't, and I figured that was probably by design — on her part. "I don't think I'm on her top-ten list."

"You never know with females. They surprise you all the time."

"Since when did you get to be such an expert on girls?"

Ryan shrugged. "There are some things I just know."

"Oh yeah, like what?"

"Like that — that stuff about girls surprising you."

I stomped hard in a snowdrift. "If Valerie wants anything to do with me ever again, I'll be more than surprised."

We had reached the school and were climbing the stairs. "Maybe she just needs a little incentive," suggested Ryan.

"What kind of incentive?"

"An encouraging note on her locker, say?"

I shook my head. "Don't even think about it," I told him.

But I couldn't shake Valerie from my mind all day. I hadn't seen her with any hot new boyfriend, but that didn't mean she didn't have one. In fact, I hadn't seen her at all lately. Maybe because she was spending all her time with a hot new boyfriend. I resolved to go back to trying to forget her.

Instead I concentrated on my hockey. Or at least I tried to. We were up against the Panthers and Cory Martinson, and the whole idea of Valerie having a boyfriend made me snarly. "Wow Swystun, where'd that intensity come from?" observed Knowles after our first shift. "Great shift!" In fact, we had a great period and came off with a two-goal lead.

"Nice work, Joel," shouted Neal, coming into the dressing room behind me. He glanced around to see if Knowles was in yet. "Did you take a double dose of the stuff last night?"

"Actually, I didn't take any." The words were out before I'd even realized what I'd said.

"What do you mean?" asked Justin.

"I forgot," I said weakly, looking around at the guys. "I mean, there's probably still enough in my system from last game."

That seemed to satisfy them.

We dropped the subject as Knowles joined us. But we didn't drop our fast-skating, quick-shooting style of hockey that was beating the Panthers. They got a lucky goal halfway through the second period, but we were already up by three at that stage and there was no way they were going to catch us. We played defensive hockey in the third period until the buzzer sounded.

"Are you skating tomorrow morning?" Ryan asked when I called to tell him the news.

"I think I'll give it a miss. I'm pretty wiped."

"That's understandable," he said. "You played tonight."

That wouldn't have stopped Ryan and I knew it, but then I wasn't Ryan. Still, I'd played a good game tonight, thanks to Valerie. I thought about calling her for about half a second, but Lise was on the phone anyway.

Still, I couldn't seem to get Valerie out of my mind. Every time Lise mentioned the skating showcase or I saw her friends, she came floating back into my head. On the way into school the next day, I took the long way through the hallway her locker was in, but didn't even catch a glimpse of her.

I was contemplating the whole thing when Ryan came racing down the hall. "You're late," I said. The first bell had just rung.

Ryan dumped his skates into his locker, grabbed his books and slammed the door shut. "He was at the rink this morning!" he exclaimed.

I was already heading to class. "Who?" Just then the late bell rang and I sprinted off, Ryan running in the other direction.

"I'll tell you at lunch," he hollered over his shoulder.

"Phil Keefler was at the rink this morning?" I echoed, my sandwich halfway to my mouth. "Why?"

Ryan shrugged. "He said he came for a skate."

"At 6:30 in the morning?"

"Yeah. I think this must have been what he was talking about — you know about helping out as an assistant coach of sorts. We were the only ones there." Ryan crushed his milk carton. "You should come next time."

I made a mental note to do just that.

But the bed was the perfect temperature when the alarm went off at 5:45 two days later. One look at Ryan that morning told me I should have gone. Phil Keefler had been there again. "Boy, the guys aren't going to believe this," I said over lunch.

"Did you tell anyone?" asked Ryan.

"Not yet," I said. "Why?"

"Nothing, really. It's kind of nice having the whole rink to ourselves. He's got some great moves, you know."

I studied Ryan again. I hadn't seen him this upbeat since his dad had decided to pull his mom out of the home. I decided to keep my mouth shut about Phil Keefler. "How are the ribs?" I asked.

"I can feel them once in a while when I skate, but I think they're on the mend. I've got to go back and see the doctor in another week or so."

"I hope he lets you come back early. We could use you," I said, recalling our last game. We had gone up by two early, but only just held on to the tie.

"You guys are doing okay."

I chewed thoughtfully. "How's your mom doing?" Ryan hadn't said much about her lately and I hadn't asked.

"Good!" said Ryan. "The doctors seem to have a handle on her diet and doses. It'll be a while before we really know if the treatment's going to work though." He paused. "Phil says that everybody reacts differently to medication, so there's no way of knowing until you try."

I raised my eyebrows. Maybe that's why Ryan hadn't said much about his mom lately. Maybe he'd found another confidante.

"I'm going up to see her after school. That's about the only good thing about not being able to play these days. I get more time at the hospital."

"Does she know you?"

Ryan shrugged. "Hard to know. Still, she seems more content, you know, more peaceful."

Lise smiled when I relayed Ryan's information. "That's great!" she said. "It's nice to know someone is."

I looked sideways at her. "How about you? Are you going crazy trying to keep your New Year's resolutions?"

She sighed. "Almost. I think I might if it wasn't for this showcase."

"Oh yeah, how's that going? Come up with any more lunch-box specials?"

She shook her head. "No, the girls were about as excited about that as you were. We're working on some other plans."

"Like?"

"Sorry, that's still confidential information." She grinned. "But you'll be the first to know when it's public knowledge."

"That's a cop-out."

"Maybe, but let's just say that we're working on something that will help you guys appreciate synchronized skating and the girls appreciate hockey more."

Lise wasn't saying anything else and all I could do was imagine what a mind like hers, left to scheme, might come up with. I dropped my books on my desk and stared at the little slip of paper tucked underneath my lamp. Valerie's phone number. I should have tossed it ages ago, but I hadn't. After all, I hadn't actually seen her with anyone else. I picked up the phone and dialed before I could talk myself out of it.

"Hello," said a woman's voice.

"Can I speak to Valerie please?" I could hear my heart pounding.

"I'm sorry, she's asleep right now." The voice paused. "She just came home yesterday and she's still very tired."

"Home?"

"Yes, she's been in the hospital."

"In the hospital?" No wonder I hadn't seen her at school.

"With meningitis, but she's much better now." The voice paused again. "Can I give her a message?"

Meningitis? I'd heard of it. "No, no thank you. I'm sorry. I didn't know she was sick," I stammered.

"It all happened rather suddenly."

"I hope she feels better," I managed before hanging up.

I sat staring at the receiver. Valerie had been in the hospital and I hadn't even known. I could have sent her flowers or something. I was still staring at the receiver when Ryan called.

"Hey Joel, guess what? You're never going to believe this." There appeared to be quite a few things I couldn't believe these days. "Mom looked at me today. When I first walked in and said hello, she looked up just like she knew me." He paused. "It didn't last long, but I swear she knew who I was."

"That's great!" I said. "How's the treatment going?"

"I didn't see the doctor, today. And the nurses always just say she's doing fine."

I tried to picture Mrs. Davis in the hospital. Maybe it was the same hospital Valerie had been in. "Valerie was in the hospital with meningitis," I blurted out.

"What? How did you find that out?"

"I called her. Her mom told me." At least I thought it was her mom.

"Wow! What are you going to do?"

"What do you mean?"

"Well, you should do something, don't you think?"

"Like what?"

"I don't know. Send her flowers or something?"

"I guess. I thought you sent those to the hospital."

Ryan considered this for a moment. "Maybe a card or something?"

Just then Dad hollered up to me. He wanted to call Angie before he went out. "I have to go. I'll think about it."

And I did, all night long, while I should have been thinking about my homework. Finally, Lise stuck her head in my room and informed me that it was getting late. She was already in the teal housecoat Dad had given her and the colour looked great on her.

"Do we have any of those sympathy cards?" I asked, trying to sound casual.

"Sympathy cards? Did someone die?"

"No, you know, the kind you send when someone's sick."

"Oh, you mean get-well cards." She disappeared and I could hear her rummaging in the cupboard. She came back with a box full of cards. "Who's it for?" she asked.

I debated about saying anything. The last thing I needed was Lise harassing me about a girl, especially a girl who possibly didn't want anything to do with me. "A friend who was in the hospital with meningitis."

Lise winced. "Ooh, that can be pretty serious," she said, leafing through the cards. "Was it bad?"

"Yeah, I guess so."

Lise threw a few cards on my bed. "Sending a card's pretty thoughtful." She pointed at the cards. "Do you like any of those?"

I looked at the windmills, sailboats and race cars on the fronts of the cards. "Don't you have anything with flowers or . . . " I didn't have the faintest idea what they put on get-well cards.

She dug back in the box. "You didn't tell me it was for a girl," she said matter-of-factly. "How's this one?" She held up one with a cute forest scene on it.

"Thanks," I said, taking the card from her. I wondered if she knew that I was just as thankful for her not making a big deal about it.

"If you address it, I'll mail it tomorrow," said Lise on the way out.

Address it? I didn't even know where Valerie lived. I traipsed downstairs and opened the phone book to the Shermans. There must have been a hundred of them. So much for that idea.

Dad came into the kitchen just as I was heading up to bed. "It's getting late, Joel. You'd better get some sleep, especially if you're coming with me early tomorrow."

I looked up quizzically at him.

"Didn't you say that you wanted to skate before school?" He rubbed his eyes. "In fact, I think I'd better get some sleep tonight, as well. I've had this horrible headache all day."

Ryan hadn't said anything about skating tomorrow, but I knew he'd be there. We did have a practice tomorrow night though. Still, there was always the chance that Phil Keefler would show up in the morning.

But even Phil Keefler couldn't make me roll out of bed an hour and a half earlier than usual. And it was just as well, because when I did head down for breakfast, Lise informed me that Dad wasn't up either. He'd been up half the night with a wicked headache. "I hope it's not that flu they've got in the states," Lise said, throwing the newspaper down in front of me. "It's already killed twenty-two people."

I glanced at the article. "It doesn't say anything about having it in Canada."

"Not yet."

"It probably wouldn't survive here anyway," I pointed out. "Look at the temperature." It had dropped to -31°C last night. I got to school just as Ryan arrived, his skates slung over his shoulder.

"Should have come, Swystun. Phil's been showing me some good moves."

"Next time," I shouted after him. But the cold spell remained and the idea of getting up early to brave the freezing cold temperatures was just too much for me. Besides, things were busy. Dad was back at work, Angie got home for a weekend and Lise was obviously up to something because she was always dashing off to meetings, making notes and answering phone calls. Between practices, games and weekly meetings, I was having trouble just fitting my schoolwork in.

Ryan was spending as much time as possible at the hospital with his mom and things seemed to be on the upswing. "Joel, she knows me!" he proclaimed one day at lunch. "I'm absolutely positive."

"Has she said anything to you?"

"Not yet, but Phil says these things take time."

I scrutinized Ryan. He *had* found another confidante and I supposed I ought to feel relieved, but I didn't. Things were different for Ryan now and somehow I wasn't a part of it. Maybe it was just that we hadn't played together for so long. In fact, I'd hardly seen Ryan outside of school. There wasn't any need for him to pick up his stuff if he wasn't playing and the doctors had told him he had to wait at least another week to practise. I shifted uneasily. Things would be back to normal as soon as he was back on the ice.

In the meantime, he kept me posted on his mom's progress and I kept him up-to-date on how the Falcons were doing without him. We'd tied a game that we should have won, but at least we hadn't lost any more. Things were looking really good for a shot at the city championships and it was the talk of our weekly meetings.

"Here's to a near-perfect record," roared Jared, raising his glass over the remnants of the pizza. We clinked glasses.

"Here's to Swystun," exclaimed Scott, toasting me. "Here's to Swystun and his magic stuff." The guys chuckled and I felt my insides flip-flop like they did every time I touched the Sinus Minus box, handed out the little zip-lock bags or even thought about it. Valentine's Day was only two weeks away.

"Joel, she smiled at Dad today!" Joel's voice was wild with excitement. "She smiled at him, Joel. And you know what else?" He continued before I could reply. "She refused to eat her green beans tonight."

I sat silently on the other end of the phone trying to digest this last bit of information.

Ryan laughed. "Mom hates green beans, always has. She pushed them away today. Wouldn't eat them and wouldn't let the nurse feed her any." He paused. "She's coming back, Joel. I just know it."

I marvelled at the change in Ryan over the past few weeks. His mom had a lot to do with it, but it was more than that. He seemed to have developed a new optimism about life, even without his hockey, and I was pretty sure that had something to do with Phil Keefler. Tomorrow, no matter what, I was going to make that early skate.

And I did. Dad dropped me at the arena on his way to work. "How are you going to skate with your eyes closed?" he asked.

I didn't answer. I was already late, but it didn't matter. None of the other guys ever showed up. I staggered into the arena. Ryan and Phil were at centre ice, doing some kind of one-on-one drill. Phil pointed to the puck, waved his arms a few times in circles and then squared off against Ryan. I watched transfixed as Ryan shadowed Phil, never losing him no matter how many dekes or turns he made. Finally Phil stopped at centre ice. Ryan flashed his trademark grin and the rink men, who had been watching from behind the glass, applauded. I knew right there and then that I wasn't going to make this morning skate either. It would take me weeks to learn to shadow a man like that. After all, it had taken Phil weeks to teach Ryan. I turned and headed for the doors. With any luck the library would be open and I could catch a few zee's in a cubicle.

CHAPTER 14

Lise was busier than ever with the skating showcase just a month away. The phone rang incessantly, but at least I wasn't stacking shoeboxes anymore. She'd become a regular hockey fan and I was amazed at the transformation.

"Lise really seems keen on this skating weekend of yours," Dad remarked over dinner one night after Lise had raced off to a meeting of some sort. "Do you guys know who's on the Old-timers' team yet?"

"No, but Knowles has been talking about doing some power skating. I think he figures that we're going to have to out-skate them if we're going to have a hope."

Dad smirked. "He's probably right." He chewed thoughtfully. "It should be an interesting game."

I wasn't sure if "interesting" was the right adjective, but it was definitely going to be fun. Ryan called that night to say that the doctor had given him the okay to practise and I could hardly wait to have him back out there. But apprehension overshadowed my excitement. Now, there was no reason not to wean the guys off the Sinus Minus — no reason at all.

"Coach Knowles called last night," Lise informed me over breakfast. "His father's very ill. He's got that bad flu and I guess he's quite elderly. Coach Knowles is trying to get a flight out to St. John's tomorrow." My spoonful of Shreddies hovered above my bowl. "Mr. Turnbull is going to take over the coaching until he's back." Mr. Turnbull had been our coach two years ago before he'd retired. Lise sipped her coffee.

"How long's he going to be gone for?" I asked, feeling my stomach sink.

"It's hard to say. I guess it depends on what happens." She smiled at me. "Oh, and you can do me a favour. Tell the guys there's a power-skating practice at Sarcee tomorrow at 4:45."

"Sarcee?" I echoed. "We never play there, and we never play right after school."

Lise shrugged. "I'm just passing on messages. I can drive, by the way."

Some of the guys had already heard the news when I got to school. It wasn't going to be easy playing under a different coach. The mood was grim as we shuffled down to the cafeteria.

Ryan elbowed me in the ribs. "Hey, isn't that Valerie?" he whispered. I followed his gaze across the cafeteria. It was Valerie all right, but either she hadn't seen me or didn't want to. "Why don't you go say hello."

I snorted. "Right, you'd just like to see me wearing her soup, wouldn't you?"

"You never know, Swystun, you just never know."

"You're coming in?" I said to Lise as she parked the van at Sarcee. "It's just a power-skating practice." I couldn't believe that Lise had become so fanatical about hockey that she was going to start watching our practices. "We're not even going to be in full equipment."

She shrugged. "Thought I'd stick around."

Ryan and I joined the team in the dressing room. We laced up our skates, threw on our jerseys and headed out as the Zamboni finished up. "Who's taking the practice?" asked Adrian. "I haven't seen Turnbull."

None of us had. Scott pulled the lock on the gate back towards him just as a group of girls came through the other gate. "Hey, what's going on?" Red queried. "Somebody double-book the ice?"

I could see Lise's curls bobbing up and down in the penalty box. She was talking to a woman wearing a yellow ski jacket. She waved the girls onto the ice as we stepped out. "Hey, isn't that the synchronized skating team we saw that day?" asked Scott.

My eyes scanned the girls, catching sight of Valerie's long, braided hair. "Yep, sure is," I muttered.

Ryan glanced sideways. "You never know, Swystun."

We skated out, wondering what was going on. The lady in the yellow ski jacket was already calling the girls in when Lise blasted a whistle and waved us over. I cringed. Surely she wasn't going to take the practice.

She climbed up onto the bench and clapped her hands. The other lady joined her and we stood staring or trying not to stare at the girls beside us. "Move closer everybody," instructed the lady. "I won't have a voice left if you stand back there."

I looked in Valerie's direction and caught her eye, but she turned away immediately. Well, that answered that question.

"Now, you're probably wondering what we're all doing here," said the lady in the yellow jacket. We murmured. "Actually, this is all part of trying to prepare for the skating showcase." I dug the heel of my skate into the ice. "Since you're all going to be on the same ice surface, and you all need to practise, we thought we might as well double up on the ice time a little bit, get to know each other."

The girls giggled and some of the guys snickered. I shifted from one foot to the other and nudged Ryan. "Lise's idea," I said as the lady continued.

"My name is Carol Lochearn. I'm the girls' synchronized skating coach and I'll be running the practice." The guys chuckled. "I'm sure you boys will know most of the drills, but if you don't the girls will be happy to show you, won't you ladies?" A couple of the girls blushed. Valerie stood with her back toward me.

"We'll start with some basic forward stroking in a figure eight. Six laps, then cut to circle thrusts, changing at the middle. Karen, you lead."

A tall brunette skated off, her arms held out to the side, her back straight. The rest of the team followed. Scott gave Neal a friendly push. "After you, Neal," he said feigning politeness, "and don't forget to hold your arms just so." We laughed, but joined in the parade.

"Pick it up," hollered Carol as Karen glided by her a second time. "And I want to see deep knee bends on those thrusts." Karen stepped up the pace and I was amazed at how quickly she and the other girls covered the ice surface. After six laps of circle thrusts, I was starting to feel my legs and I expect the other guys were too, because they had stopped joking around. We assembled in front of

Carol. Valerie skated to the opposite side and eyed me angrily. "Good work. Now, backward circle thrusts on all four corner circles using the centre circle for transition."

The guys looked around puzzled as Karen headed out to the closest circle. We followed the girls, but only our defencemen could keep up with them on the backwards drill. We dug in and managed to hang on. "Don't lose that momentum," hollered Carol. "Remember to keep that balance point, especially on this next turn drill."

"Jolene and Taryn, maybe you girls had better demo this one," she said. "I want the turns on the lines with squats between." Two of the girls broke away from the group and made a lap of the ice. "Start on the centre line," screamed Carol. We watched as the girls hit the red line, turned backwards into a squat, stood up and turned seconds before the blue line, dropping into another squat. "The important thing here is balance," Carol told us. "If you don't find that balance point, you'll be down in seconds."

The girls took off with the Falcons right behind them. "That old broad doesn't think we can do this," murmured Justin, "but watch this." He hit the centre line and turned into a low squat, barely hanging on to a sitting position. About six of us managed the first turn, but by the second turn almost all of us were lying on the ice. Only Geordie, our goalie, managed the whole rink. The girls applauded as he made it back to the bench and bowed. We slapped him on the back, all of us laughing now.

"Maybe we had better back up a few steps," grinned Carol. "Let's start with some basic turns." She pointed to Neal. "You there, show me a three turn." We turned to stare at Neal.

"Is that different from a four turn?" he asked, and we exploded into laughter. The girls were laughing now and so were Carol and Lise.

"How about if we divide into four groups, guys and girls, and maybe we can review three turns." Carol clapped her hands. "Let's go, people."

Valerie skated towards the far corner with a friend. "Want to head in that direction?" Ryan asked.

"No thanks. I've already had a few killing looks." I skated off to another corner, Ryan at my side.

The girls were pretty good instructors and in about five minutes we had the three turns down. They weren't really so hard, just a lot cleaner than the two-footed turns most of us used.

"Okay, let's try that last drill again," hollered Carol pointing towards our group. "Group one, you start."

We skated off, guys and girls together, trying to remember our balance point, and actually fared a little better. Alex and I went down on the last turn, but Ryan, Dave and Adrian made it all the way. By the time the rest of the groups had joined us, we were all mingling about and talking.

Carol blew the whistle and we went silent. "Well done. Now, we have another little surprise for you." She motioned over her shoulder at Lise. "This is Lise Harper-Swystun. She's one of the mothers who have been trying to organize the skating showcase. Remember, this could be a big fundraiser for both teams." We stood silently, thinking of

Denver. "This could be an annual event, but it all depends on how successful this year's show is." She paused. "There will be some solo figure skaters, the girls will be doing a few numbers and the Falcons will be playing some old NHL players. But the committee has been tossing around a few other 'fun' ideas as well." She smiled. "I'll let Lise tell you about them."

Lise fidgeted. I couldn't even imagine what she was going to say. "As Carol mentioned, the purpose of the weekend is to showcase our skating talents and to entertain the crowd. So, we felt that adding a little humour to the program might be a good idea." She stopped. "Now, I know that all of you here can skate, so we thought it might be fun to let the girls play a little hockey and let the guys try their hand at synchronized skating." A wave of exclamations swept through the group.

Lise blew the whistle and took a deep breath. "The idea is to let the girls do a few numbers, then on the final one, when they come off to change, send the Falcons out to do the finale."

We laughed. There wasn't much else to do but laugh.

"Do they have to wear our costumes?" asked Karen, eyeing Scott.

"I think it would be a lot more effective if they did," answered Lise.

A couple of the guys shook their heads and all of us shifted uneasily.

Scott stared back at Karen. "And the girls are going to play hockey?" he asked smirking.

"That's the idea," said Lise. "We haven't sorted out the details, but we'd like to do it all without Coach Knowles knowing. I think we'll put them on with five minutes or so left in the third period."

"In hockey equipment?" asked Jared.

"Again, I think that would be most effective."

The girls giggled.

"So," shouted Lise, "what do you all say?"

We stood silently, staring at our teammates and the others.

"What do you think, guys?" asked Neal surveying all of us. "It might be fun."

Carl lunged forward. "Are you out of your mind? Like it's going to be fun parading around as girls doing some fancy figure skating thing?"

Scott shrugged, then glanced at Karen. "Yeah."

"Yeah," said a couple of the other guys and soon, except for Carl, there was a general murmur of consent.

"We're game if you are," said Scott, turning back to eye Karen.

Karen blushed. She glanced around at her teammates. "What do you think?" The girls' camp buzzed excitedly. "Why not!" announced Karen, turning to face us.

Lise clapped her hands together and grinned the broadest grin I'd ever seen. I was smiling too, although I wasn't sure why. In fact, almost all the guys and girls had smiles on their faces. I tried to catch a glimpse of Valerie, but she was hidden behind some taller girls.

"All right," Carol said, raising her voice above the din, "if we're going to pull this off, we're going to have to get to work." She cleared her throat. "From what I've seen so far, the Falcons could stand to learn a few things about synchronized skating, and I'm pretty sure that the girls could learn a thing or two about hockey." The din surged again.

"Next time we meet — and I believe Lise has a schedule for you — if you fellas could bring an extra hockey stick along, we'll work on the hockey skills. But for right now, we've got another half hour to try to teach you klutzes a thing or two."

The girls laughed while we held our heads high, pretending to be hurt by the insult.

"I want you all to divide into groups of four — two girls, two guys. Don't get too fussy. We'll be rotating constantly. Introduce yourselves and we'll start by having the girls explain a basic line manoeuvre."

Ryan and I paired off with two girls named Carla and Pauline. In no time, the four of us were doing basic line and circle manoeuvres all linked together. Then Carol put two groups together and gradually we built up into a massive line. We started at one end of the rink and manoeuvered our way down, criss-crossing behind and re-attaching to the opposite end. It took a bit of getting used to, but even Carol had to admit that we weren't as clumsy as we looked.

"Concentric circles," ordered Carol. "Girls in the middle, guys on the outside. Face your partner." Carol put us through a few different holds and basic stationary steps, moving the outside circle so that we changed partners each time.

"There'll be a quiz at the end of the practice," she called. "You all have to know each other's names."

I rolled my eyes. I'd met so many girls in the last twenty minutes, I didn't have a clue who half of them were. The red-haired girl in front of me spun off and I found myself face to face with Valerie. "Well, at least I'll know your name," I said, trying to lighten things up.

She looked away while we waited for Carol's next instructions.

"I guess you're pretty mad at me," I said, suddenly feeling the urge to explain. "About the Christmas dance and all."

She threw a cold glare in my direction while Carol and Lise fiddled with the music system.

"I never saw you to explain," I said. "But actually, I had a perfectly good reason for not showing up that night."

She looked skeptical. "Yeah?"

I looked up quickly at the sound of her voice. She was waiting. "You see, I was going to meet Ryan and go from there, but when I got to his house, his mom had tried to commit suicide and we ended up at the hospital. I couldn't just leave him there and it took a while to sort things out. By the time my dad came and got me, I was pretty exhausted. I guess I just wasn't up to a dance." I glanced up at Valerie who was staring straight into my eyes. I shifted from one skate to the other. "I, I'm sorry I didn't call and explain," I said. "See, I . . . " My voice trailed off. I didn't see any point in asking about her new boyfriend.

Valerie said nothing.

"Then, I meant to see you at school, but you were sick. I, uh, I found out when I called, but you were already home by then and I tried to send you a card, but there's about 100 Shermans in the book and . . . " I stopped, suddenly realizing how stupid I sounded. Valerie was still staring at me, when the music blared. I jumped and looked in Carol's direction. "Anyway," I muttered, "I can't blame you for being mad."

"Okay, I'd like everyone to pair off — one guy, one girl — and line up on the red line at that end of the rink," directed Carol, pointing to the far end. I looked around for Ryan, but he was already engaged in conversation with a petite, dark-haired girl whose name, I thought, was Taryn.

"Hey Valerie," Justin called skating by, "want to be my partner?"

I turned my back and started to skate towards the sidelines where a few of the other guys had assembled. "No thanks, Justin. I'm already paired up with Joel."

I stopped at the sound of my name and looked back over my shoulder.

"I think," she added, looking in my direction.

I retraced my steps as Justin skated off in search of another partner. "You mean, you're still speaking to me?" I asked.

"I wasn't," she admitted, "but I should have known something had happened the night of the dance when neither you nor Ryan showed up." She rubbed her palms together. "I saw Theo in the mall one day and I was going to

248

ask him, but I was with my cousin and . . . well, I didn't."

I looked up. At least that answered my question about her having a boyfriend.

She smiled warmly at me. "I had no idea, Joel. What a story."

"It's true!"

Her voice softened. "I know. Nobody could make that up. It must have been horrible."

"It was," I said, recalling that night in the hospital, "especially for Ryan."

We skated towards the others on the red line and joined Ryan and Taryn. Ryan elbowed me in the ribs as Carol started giving instructions. "See," he whispered, "you never know."

CHAPTER 15

By the end of the second practice, I had to admit that Ryan had been right. Valerie and I were partners whenever possible during practices and having a blast. In fact, the whole team was having a great time and we were even making a little progress. The girls were trying to teach us a quick, easy, Mexican number and we were desperately trying to educate them about shooting pucks, stickhandling and staying onside.

"They're actually pretty good skaters," Neal noted over lunch one day. "But boy, they've got hands of lead."

"I know," agreed Justin. "Every time Brenda's stick touched the puck, the two parted company. I think we're going to have to resort to crazy glue."

"Did you see Jennifer's shot?" asked Pete.

"The one from the top of the goal crease that ended up behind her?" asked Red. "It was almost as good as Kate's."

"At least hers went in," I noted.

"Yeah, but only because she kicked it in."

"Personally, I think we should take their sticks away from them and let them play with their feet," said Ryan. He rubbed a cut above his eyebrow. "They're downright dangerous with those things."

Geordie joined us at the table. "Hey guys, guess what? I just heard that Knowles will be back for tonight's practice." We hammered the table.

"Great!" exclaimed Jared.

"At least Turnbull held us in there without any losses," said Tony.

"No, the stuff held us in there," whispered Adrian. "And it's going to take us to the city champs too."

I looked away. Ryan pushed his chair abruptly back from the table. "Gotta' go," he said.

"What's wrong with him?" asked Scott.

I shrugged, but inside me I had this terrible feeling that I knew. Ryan wasn't keen on me supplying the guys. I watched him take the stairs two at a time. And it wasn't really all that surprising — not with his history and his mom and all. I looked at my watch. February 4th. I had ten days.

Knowles was into making up for lost time and he worked us hard. I was wiped by the end of the week as Ryan and I walked out to the bus stop. "You coming to the meeting tonight?" I asked.

Ryan stiffened up. "No," he said, "I'm going up to see Mom instead. I haven't seen her much this week."

"How's she doing?"

"Good! She seems to know us more these days, but she still doesn't talk to anybody."

"It's a start."

"Yeah." He kicked violently at some frozen snow in front of us. "At least the doctors seem to know what they're doing. Fooling around with drugs and not knowing what they might do in the long term is pretty risky." He eyed me as Neal and Dave caught up with us. That sinking feeling took hold of me again.

I didn't offer Ryan any stuff for our game that weekend and he didn't ask. It didn't seem to affect Ryan's game. He got two goals, Theo got one, and we walked away with a 3-0 win over the Blades.

Knowles was busy planning our futures. "I'm going to have to cancel Thursday's practice this week," he told us after the game. "I'll be away on business. But I've managed to get some ice time at Renfrew right after school on Wednesday."

Our heads snapped up and we looked around the room. That was the same time as our synchronized skating practice. "But that's our practice for — ouch!" muttered Neal, as Dave kicked him in the shins. We stared hard at him.

"Uh, we can't make it that night," said Scott finally.

"We?" asked Knowles. "How many of you can't be there?"

Slowly our hands went up, one after another. "All of you?" asked Knowles suspiciously. "What's going on?"

Neal cleared his throat. "We've got this practice thing . . . " He looked around desperately.

"With a bunch of kids from school," added Adrian, trying not to lie.

Knowles frowned. "Practice for what?"

"Uh, it's a presentation . . . " began Scott

" . . . for the parents," I added quickly.

Knowles studied us curiously. "All right," he said finally. "Then I want everyone at the early morning skate on Thursday. We'll use it as practice time."

We let out a collective sigh of relief. "Sure, sure," we muttered and filed out the door.

"Neal almost let the cat out of the bag tonight," I told Lise after we'd dropped Ryan off. "He just about told Knowles about the synchronized skating sessions."

"Uh-oh. I'm not sure he'd go for that. I think he'd be worried that you guys might not be so focused on your hockey."

Lise was right. Knowles didn't know anything about our synchronized skating rehearsals, but he certainly thought we were losing our focus. We heard about it at Thursday's early morning practice.

"Knowles has a point," said Ryan as we walked down the road to school. "We've got to stay focused if we're going to beat the Cadillacs and especially if we're going to play well in Denver."

Theo poked Tony in the ribs. "No more fancy 360s in warm-up. You're going to give us away for sure."

We laughed. "Remember, we're just trading in our jerseys for dresses once, not on a regular basis."

"I can hardly wait," moaned Carl. Tonight was the night we got our costumes. Lise and some of the other parents had been busy altering them.

"Have you seen them, Swystun?" asked Red.

"No, but Lise says they're colourful and revealing!"

"If Lise thinks they're colourful, we're really in trouble," groaned Ryan.

"Ooooh," shrieked Neal in a high-pitched voice as we turned into the schoolyard. "I'm so excited."

In fact we were all pretty excited. So excited that we even joined Valerie and a couple of other girls from the team for lunch. That suited me just fine and I even managed to sit beside her. "What colour are they?" quizzed Pete.

"All different colours — reds, greens, oranges, blues, pinks."

"Oh, I hope I get pink," cooed James, "it's my absolute favourite."

Red smoothed back his long mane of hair. "Well, personally, I think I'm an autumn — orange or green please."

Simone laughed. "And they're low-cut."

Pete held his chin in his hands and rolled his eyes to the ceiling. "I hope my bra strap doesn't show," he said.

Carl groaned and put his head down on the table.

"And they're skin tight," noted Valerie.

"You mean everyone's going to see my chest?" asked Scott, pretending to be nervous.

I looked at Scott and his well-developed pectorals. He didn't have anything to be worried about. "Are you serious?" I asked Valerie in a whisper.

"Yes," she whispered back.

"Do we have to wear those party hose things?" asked Tony suddenly. Simone's drink went down the wrong way and Valerie had to hit her on the back. "They're called panty hose," Simone explained, still coughing. "But I think we had to wear fishnet stockings for that number, didn't we?"

Valerie nodded as we erupted into a chorus of groans. "And feathers in our hair."

"I'd rather die," complained Carl as the bell rang.

"Well I can hardly wait," shrieked Pete.

It was true. We could hardly wait and we were all in great spirits, with the possible exception of Carl, when we arrived at the rink. A couple of moms arrived carrying hangers full of costumes, and deposited them in the dressing room. There would be time for costumes at the end of the practice. But first, Carol was intent on making sure we knew what we were doing on the ice.

"Now, we've only got a few practices left, guys, and we don't want you looking like fools out there," she told us.

"Somehow, I think that's a given," muttered Carl.

"We're going to go through it piece by piece with the music today. The girls will help you in your groups. Then, hopefully, we'll be ready to try it all together." Carol picked up the tape. "Remember, it's a Mexican number. It's snappy and quick, terse and short, so let's keep it that way."

We split into our groups and worked hard. There were five basic sequences to remember: a diamond block, a diagonal line, a V intersection, concentric circles and a three-spoke wheel. Each one consisted of different holds and footwork sequences and it took a lot of hard work and concentration to pull it off. "All right," shouted Carol as the music stopped. "We still have to work on straightening out those lines, but it's coming. We'll have to tighten that up next practice." She smiled at us. "Now I think the moms want to see the fellows for outfitting. Girls, you're free to go."

Lise gave us each an outfit and told us to come out for a fitting inspection when we were ready.

Inside the dressing room we stood looking at our dresses.

"This is nuts!" complained Carl. "I'm not putting this on."

Ryan fingered his neon green outfit. "They're kind of bright."

"Nobody's going to miss us, that's for sure," said Jared, eyeing his own fluorescent-orange dress.

"Well," said Scott taking his off the hanger. "Might as well get it over with." He struggled into his dress, while the rest of us took ours reluctantly off the hangers. "Are these ever tight," muttered Scott, trying to pull up the shoulders. "There!" He stood in the centre of the dressing room in his teal dress, and it was too much for the rest of us.

We erupted into fits of laughter, collapsed on the benches and rolled on the floor.

"How's it going in there?" asked Lise's voice from the door.

"Just fine," sang out Neal. "We'll be out in a second."

Scott studied his image in the mirror while Adrian walked around him. "They weren't kidding when they said they were low cut," he observed. "I can see your navel."

Scott pulled his spandex top up. "I'd like to see the girls in these," he commented, smoothing down the hair on his chest and doing up the small silky rope button under his chin.

"Yeah," we all agreed as we struggled into our dresses. We'd definitely like to see the girls in these! About ten minutes later, we were all outfitted and ready to go.

"I can hardly breathe," muttered Theo, tugging at his dress. "How am I supposed to skate?"

"How are you doing, boys?" asked Lise's voice again. "Come on out when you're done and we'll see if we need to make any alterations."

Jared twirled in front of the mirror. "Don't you just love the way these skirts flair?" he said, pushing one hip out seductively.

A couple of the guys tried a few quick twirls, their skirts swirling high around their waists. Carl slapped his forehead with his palms.

"Let's go, guys," advised Lise.

"Come on," urged Neal. He manoeuvered his way to the door and thrust his head out. "You first," he said, suddenly pushing Adrian to the front.

"After you," said Adrian, shoving Tony in front of him.

"Ladies first," grinned Tony, giving Pete a nudge.

"I'll go first," announced Scott. He strode to the front of the line and peeked around the corner. "The girls are all here still," he whispered ducking back in.

"Oh no," we moaned.

Pete stuck his head around the corner. "Then there's only one thing to do — we'll have a parade." And shoving Scott aside, he marched out of the dressing room. We followed, marching in a long line, clear down to the lobby and around it twice before Pete called a halt. The girls were all howling and clapping by the time we'd stopped.

Valerie made her way to me. "You've, you've all," she managed between gasps of laughter, "you've all got them on backwards."

I could feel the colour rise in my face and hear Ryan moan behind me as Taryn imparted the same information to him. "Listen up, boys, please," called Lise, trying to gain control of her laughter. "You do indeed all have the dresses on backwards . . . "

"But I like it," announced Carol. "Let them show a little hairy cleavage."

The girls agreed and we relaxed.

Carol surveyed the group of us. "Besides, you'll look much better in fishnet stockings." She glanced at Lise. "I'll let you moms check for alterations and the girls can give out the feathers." The girls disappeared onto the bleachers and came back with huge feathers of matching colours.

"How are we supposed to keep these on?" asked James, running a hand over his buzz cut.

"You'll need a headband, James," advised Carol. "The rest of you might manage with combs and bobby pins."

I winced as Valerie stabbed my head with a bobby pin. "Easy eh?"

She smiled. "I need to put another one in the front and then it should hold."

I looked down at the curves of her hips as her hair fell forward onto my shoulders and fought an urge to wrap my arms around her. Instead, I caught her hand as she stepped back. "Thanks," I said, bouncing my feather back and forth.

She gave me a radiant smile. "You look terrific! Red suits you!"

"The girls will go over makeup later this — "

We burst into exclamations. "Makeup?" echoed Carl. I remembered Valerie's face the day I'd run into her in the corridor.

"We'll go over that next time we meet," announced Carol. "Please leave your costumes with me or give them to Lise if they need to be altered. And guys, remember your equipment next time please."

This time the girls groaned.

"I've got to go," said Valerie, glancing into the parking lot. "I'll see you at school tomorrow." She grinned at me. "You look terrific — really," she added before bursting into laughter.

"Yeah, well, I can't wait to see you in my hockey equipment," I called after her.

CHAPTER 16

I didn't have to wait long, just until the next practice. We had finally managed to get the girls thinking about offsides, instead of just shooting and passing. "Good job, people," Carol said. "There's only a week and a half to go, so we're going to be splitting the practice sessions — half hockey, half synchronized skating. And remember, don't breathe a word of this outside these walls. It's a surprise!" She paused. "Now, I think we're due to retire to dressing room #3 for a little demo on how to put on hockey equipment."

We filed through the corridor to our dressing room. Lise was already there, trying to make room for everyone. Valerie and Taryn squeezed in next to Ryan and me. It was a tight fit, but I for one didn't mind, and I don't think Ryan did either. He put an arm around the back of Taryn's shoulders and leaned against the wall. I followed suit and to my surprise, Valerie leaned against my shoulder.

Neal and Scott were already in the centre of the room laying out equipment. "Okay, first we'll do a little demo and then you can try." Scott reached into his bag. "This first piece of equipment," he said, wrenching something from the top of his bag, " is called a . . . " He stood stock-still holding his jockstrap as the colour flooded his face. The girls burst into laughter and Neal doubled over holding his stomach. Scott stuffed the jockstrap back into his bag and pulled out his garter belt. "The first piece of equipment *you'll* need," he began again, "is the garter belt that comes with these little clips that hold up your socks." He stepped into his belt and gave Neal a swift kick in the shin.

"Right," said Neal, clutching his shin, "belts first — right after your jockstraps." Laughter absorbed his voice.

Scott gave him a quick hip check and sent him flying into Simone's lap. She pulled him down in front of her.

"Okay," said Scott. "Next you slip your shin pads on and then pull your socks over those." In moments, he was wearing both. "Then you attach your clips to your socks like this and put on your hockey pants." He clipped on his socks, stepped into his pants and pulled his suspenders over his shoulders. "Those are followed by shoulder pads and elbow pads," he said, deftly putting them on. "Then this neck guard goes around your neck and attaches at the back. Your jersey goes on over the top." He pulled on his blue Falcons sweater. "After that you put on your skates," he said, pointing at his feet, "and your helmet and gloves." Within seconds, he was fully dressed. The girls clapped and Scott bowed all around. "Your turn," he said, sweeping the room with his hand.

Valerie struggled to her feet and unzipped my bag. Thankfully, Lise had washed my equipment. She rummaged around for my belt and put it on, pulling it tighter to make it smaller. It took her two tries to get my shin pads on right side up, but clipping on the socks was no problem. Hockey pants were straightforward, although two of us could have fit in them, but shoulder pads were another story. After three attempts, she managed to untangle her hair and get them on right way around.

"You might want to put your hair up," I told her. She had no trouble with the elbow pads. I did up the neck guard while she held her hair out of the way. A few minutes later, she was wearing my hockey sweater, helmet and gloves and looking perfectly beautiful.

"How do you skate in this stuff?" Valerie wanted to know.

The girls looked around and giggled at each other, but Lise seemed happy enough. "Naturally, you'll be in your own skates, and we've arranged for some equipment rentals for that day." She paused and looked around at the girls' baffled expressions. "Trust me," she said smiling, "you don't want to wear the boys' equipment after they've played for two periods — the jersey will be bad enough."

The girls grimaced. "Do me a favour and don't sweat," Taryn told Ryan.

"On the day of the skating showcase," Lise continued, "we're going to arrange to inter- rupt the game with about five minutes left. We haven't sorted out all the details, but the guys will have to leave the ice and when they do, you girls will have to be dressed and ready to go, minus their sweaters. You should have enough time to switch over. Guys, you're going to have to stay out of sight, at least for the first few minutes, until the Old-timers realize the girls are out there. It shouldn't take long, but don't follow the girls out."

"How are you going to get us off the ice without Knowles knowing about all this?" asked Pete.

"We're still working on that one, but we'll find a way." She glanced around at all of us. "Okay, girls, you can take off the equipment. That's it for today. Remember, Monday next week is a double practice, followed by a makeup session. We're getting down to the crunch."

"Don't worry, you'll think of something," I told Lise on the way home as she tugged on her curls. They were chocolate brown today and suited her. "Hey, I like your hair that colour," I said.

Lise's mind was elsewhere. "I hope we come up with something soon. The tricky part is getting Knowles to go one way while you guys go the other."

"What about a blackout," I suggested.

"Can't, it's against safety regulations. Something to do with the fire and safety act." Lise tilted her head to one side. "Wait a minute," she began slowly, "that might just work."

"What, the blackout?"

"No, the fire thing. What if the fire alarm went off?"

"Isn't that against the fire and safety act, too?" I asked.

"Sure, sure, but what if they were in on it? The fire department I mean?"

It had potential. "I guess so, but how are you going to separate Knowles from the team?"

Lise sighed again. "I don't know Joel. Has he ever had to leave the bench during a game?"

I thought hard. "Just once when he had a bad case of diarrhea."

Lise frowned. "Not exactly an easy solution!"

"Oh yeah, and once when some guy was trying to have his car towed."

"His car towed?"

"Yeah, I guess he parked in some emergency vehicle place or something and they were going to tow his car."

Lise grinned at me. "Joel, you're a genius!"

I wasn't feeling much like a genius when I tried my homework that night. It wasn't that it was a difficult assignment; I just couldn't concentrate. I kept feeling Valerie lean back against me and seeing her in all my equipment. I finally took a break and phoned Ryan. The line was busy. I thought about phoning Valerie, but what was I going to say? I finally got through to Ryan who was floating.

"Hey Swystun, I was just going to call you. You're never going to believe this." I opened my mouth to say something, but Ryan just kept on. "I went to see Mom today after supper, and she called me by name. She knew Dad too."

"Cool!"

"And then when I got home, Taryn called."

"She called you?"

"Yep, just called to chat I guess. She's something else."

"What did you two talk about?"

"Things. Like the costumes and equipment and a little about her school and family."

"All that tonight?"

"Yeah, it just kind of happened." I could hear Ryan's dad's voice in the background. "Anyway, I better go. I've been on the phone since we got home."

I set the receiver down and looked at the clock. It was early enough to call Valerie and I'd already memorized her number. Maybe I didn't have to have anything to say; maybe it would just happen. I picked up the phone, but Lise's voice crackled in my ear.

She burst through my door minutes later. "I'm done, if you want to make a call," she said. "And it's all arranged. The towing company is going to erect a handicapped parking sign in front of Coach Knowles' car after he's gone in and then they're going to arrange to come and tow it. When he gets word of that, he'll have to go sort it out. That's when we'll sound the fire alarm. The fire department's been great. They're going to arrive with their sirens on and do the whole routine, except that the girls and the Falcons will be allowed to remain in the building. By the time Knowles finishes with the towing company, the game will have started again and the girls will be on the ice." She stopped, out of breath.

"Wow!" I said. "You arranged all that?"

"Everyone's keen to help out a good cause." She looked hard at me. "Speaking of which, Joel, what's happening?"

I shifted uneasily.

"It's only four days until Valentine's Day," she reminded me.

"I know. We're supposed to have a meeting tomorrow night and I'm not going to take the stuff." There, I'd said it.

"What are you going to tell the guys?"

"Maybe that my supply's dried up."

"And they're going to be okay with that?"

"They'll have to be, I guess."

"It's the right thing to do, Joel." We stood in silence. "Who do you play next?"

"The Blades. We should be able to take them, although that's what I said last time."

"Still, it's got to be done."

I flopped down on my bed. "I know, I know."

Lise pointed to the phone. "It's free now, if you want to make a call." She glanced at the clock. "She'll still be up."

I blushed as the phone rang. "Hello," I said, glad of the interruption.

It was Justin with the news that Knowles' father had just passed away and he was going to have to go back to St. John's. I motioned for Lise to stick around.

"Now what am I going to do?" I asked her after I'd given her the details.

She drew her fingers across her chin.

"I'm going to have to wait until he's back, Lise. The guys will be crazy if this happens now."

"Okay," she said finally, "but as soon as he's back, regardless of who you're playing."

I swallowed hard. "But what if it's a top place team?"

"Regardless of who you're playing," Lise repeated sternly.

I gave in. "Okay, okay, regardless of who we're playing."

I didn't phone Valerie in the end. I was too busy trying to figure out who we'd have to face the first day off the stuff. It was likely to be the Chiefs and they were never easy. And that would be just days before the Old-timers' game too. This whole thing was a never-ending nightmare.

In fact, it was such a nightmare that I found myself hoping we'd lose our next game against the Blades, just so we would lose to an easy team on the stuff. But one of their forwards was out with an injury and Ryan was making moves we'd never seen before.

"Must be the synchronized skating," whispered Pete as we skated off with a 4-0 win.

"Must be," I agreed, but I'd seen those moves before — at an early morning skate with Phil Keefler.

"You made some great dekes out there tonight," I told Ryan as we headed out the arena doors.

"Thanks."

I could feel Ryan's eyes on me. "What?" I asked.

"Well, I was just thinking about something Phil told me the other day."

"About deking guys?"

"No, about deceiving guys."

I stopped in my tracks and stared at Ryan's back. "What are you talking about?" We stepped out into the darkness as Dad drove into the parking lot.

I didn't have a chance to say any more in the car, but I had this gnawing feeling in my stomach that wouldn't go away all through my shower. I called Ryan as soon as I got out. "Ryan, it's Joel." I could hear the TV in the background. "I was thinking about what you said, and I just want you to know that I've got it all under control. As soon as Knowles gets back, it's done, the stuff I mean." I stopped to catch my breath.

"I'm glad, Joel," said Ryan from the other end.

I deliberated about telling him it was Sinus Minus, but that seemed to be making a farce of the whole issue. "I'm sorry Ryan. I was going to do it earlier, but with you being hurt and Knowles' father and all, it didn't seem like the right time."

Ryan said nothing.

"Anyway, as soon as Knowles is back, that's it." I paused. "I just hope the guys don't flip out."

"We'll just have to show them we don't need it," said Ryan.

I felt relief overcome me. Ryan was on my side. "Right!" I said. "That first game off the stuff, we'll have to have the game of our lives."

"Why not? It'll be a good warm-up for the Old-timers' game. I think that's going to be a challenge."

"Me too."

"One thing though," pondered Ryan aloud. "What happens if the girls lose it for us in the last five minutes?"

I'd thought of that. "They won't count that, will they?"

"Don't know. We'll just have to make sure we're way out in front by then."

I felt better by the time I'd hung up, and so did Lise when I told her about my conversation with Ryan. "That's the best news I've had for a while," she said. "I'm glad you've made up your mind."

I was glad too. It wasn't going to be easy, but together Ryan and I could be tough to beat.

We certainly didn't look tough when the girls had finished with us at the end of the next practice. "Ouch!" exclaimed Red. "This stuff stings."

Fiona grabbed the mascara from him. "You're not supposed to stick it in your eye, just do your eyelashes like I showed you."

I stared at my reflection in the mirror. "Try putting the eyeshadow on the other eyelid," instructed Valerie. "Remember, they're supposed to match."

I rubbed the brush in the eyeshadow and tried to keep one eye shut and look at the other one.

"This is impossible," moaned Ryan beside me. "How do you trace the bottom of your eyelid without making the line all bumpy?"

"Now remember," said Lise, "you guys are going to have to do this after you get dressed."

"What about Coach Knowles?" asked Theo.

"We've already arranged to have him called out of the dressing room to do a newspaper interview during the figure skating perform-ance. Play around with your equipment if you have to, but don't change into your hockey uniforms. Once he's left, switch dressing rooms. You'll have time to dress while the girls skate. You'll also have to do makeup, so you might want to practise a little bit at home."

"That'd go over well with my dad," Pete joked.

"And my mom," added Scott. "I'd have to use her makeup."

"Never mind then, just be quick about it."

We moaned in unison.

"All the costumes will be in dressing room #4. As soon as Knowles leaves, you've got to switch rooms, get dressed and get your makeup on. Then, you've got to get out behind the black curtain that will be hanging at the south end of the rink just as the girls' second number ends." Lise's eyes swept the room. "You guys got that?"

We nodded. "Just don't be upset if my lipstick's crooked," called Theo in a high-pitched voice. "I hate to be rushed like that."

Knowles hurried back from the funeral for the big game against the Cadillacs. Luckily the guys already had their stuff for the game. We hadn't played the Cadillacs for quite a while, but we were ready, or so we thought.

"Why are they so good?" asked Simone over lunch.

"Lots of reasons," said Adrian. "They can shoot, pass, skate and check."

"Sounds like us," said Jolene.

"Not quite," drawled Red. "But at least Knowles is here." He grinned at the girls. "You coming to cheer us on tonight?"

Valerie shrugged. "Maybe, where do you play?"

"Southland Arena at 7:45."

"We could go," suggested Valerie.

"Sure, why not?" said Jolene. "It would probably be good for us to see how hockey's supposed to look."

Just then Pete joined us. He was covered in snow. "You should see it out there," he said blowing into his hands. "It's snowing like crazy. There must be twenty centimeters already and I heard it's supposed to snow all day."

By dismissal time, thirty-five centimeters of snow had fallen and the bus ride home took an extra hour and a half. By 6:00 they had closed half the roads and all the public arenas and pools. "Looks like you've got the night off," said Lise after listening to the news. "I hope Steve makes it home."

Dad made it home, but not until after 9:00. I hadn't seen snow like this ever before. By 10:00 all the schools had been shut down and 50 centimeters of the white, fluffy stuff covered the driveway. And it wasn't supposed to stop until sometime during the night. We had to dig Jasper out of his doghouse and bring him in before we went to bed, and those white flakes just kept on coming.

That meant that our game against the Cadillacs would be rescheduled, and according to Knowles, who called to let us know, it wouldn't be until just after the skating show-case next weekend. I frowned when Lise gave us the news. I'd promised Ryan and Lise I'd wean the guys off the stuff, but that would mean their first game without the stuff would be against the Cadillacs. I couldn't do that, could I?

"You certainly can," said Lise, when I told her my predicament. "And you will."

"But Lise, it's the Cadillacs."

"So what! They're just another hockey team."

"Yeah, right," I protested. "Another great hockey team."

"The key word is 'another', the Falcons being the other," Lise insisted.

"Just one more game — "

"No!" There was a finality that I'd never heard before in Lise's voice. "No Joel. It has to stop. First it was Christmas, then Valentine's, now this is it. No more."

I stared at her. How would she know if I gave out one more batch of the stuff?

"Besides, you promised Ryan."

That was the real clincher. Lise might not know, but Ryan would. I'd given Ryan my word and not keeping it might mean losing my best friend.

CHAPTER 17

Lise left and I flopped back on my bed and stared at the stucco. At least our synchronized skating routine was giving me something other than the Sinus Minus to think about. We ate lunch with the girls almost every day now. We won our game against the Chiefs mid-week and everything was falling into place, or so I thought until Justin reminded me that they were out of the stuff.

"I'm . . . I'm not sure I can get any more before the weekend," I stammered, looking at Ryan.

"What do you mean? We're playing the Old-timers."

"I know," I began.

"We won't need it anyway," added Ryan. "We're not even half their age. We can smoke 'em without it."

"That's Phil Keefler, amongst others, you're talking about," said Scott.

"What about the stuff, Joel?" asked Adrian.

"I can't get it before the weekend. I'm out!" The guys swore.

"You won't even notice you don't have it," said Ryan. "Not at a game like this."

"Hey," began Theo slowly, "didn't you play without it one day, Swystun?"

"Yes," I said truthfully.

"And you said it would last long enough to get you through an extra game."

"Yeah, that's right," added Pete. "We'll still have enough stuff in our systems from last night's game. We'll be okay."

I sighed. They'd be okay, but what about me and my predicament? And what about the game against the Cadillacs on Monday?

The girls were already in their dressing room when we arrived and found Coach Knowles.

"Pretty exciting, eh boys?" grinned Coach Knowles. "Playing these guys is going to be different than anything you've ever done before."

We unzipped our bags and made a pretense of sifting through our equipment.

"Now you know that there's no body-checking." He smiled. "I think that's more for their protection than yours, so you're going to have to be content to stick-check and tie them up along the boards. The big thing though is your skating. You've got to skate hard and make them go with you, because you're never going to outmanoeuvre them."

We looked up as the figure skating performance was announced. The knock on the door came right on cue. "I've got to step out for some newspaper interview," Knowles told us. "Hurry up and get changed. We don't have all day."

As soon as he was gone, we counted to twenty, then raced into dressing room #4. I'd managed to catch a glimpse of the girls waiting to go out onto the ice. They looked great, all decked out in Japanese kimonos with their fans and makeup.

"Hurry up," hissed Lise as she closed the door behind us.

"All right ladies," sang out Neal. "Into your costumes and don't forget these lovely fishing nets we're supposed to put on."

The costumes were all laid out, with the fishnet stockings on top. We stripped down and shoved our feet into the stockings. "Ouch, these things kill," complained Red.

"Oh no," moaned Geordie. "I've got a snag."

I was still fighting with my second leg when Ryan started jumping up and down beside me. "How do you get these things pulled up?" he asked. The crotch was almost level with his knees.

"From the ankle first," advised Jared, who had three sisters.

Ryan and I managed to get them on about the same time and dove for our costumes. "Remember to wear them backwards; we want to see that cleavage," instructed Dave.

"This is insane, absolutely insane," groaned Carl as he pulled on his skates.

Neal slapped him on the back just as the synchronized skating team was announced. "Oh no, they're already on for their first number and we still have makeup to do."

We jammed our feather combs into our hair and grabbed our cosmetic bags. Lise had hung mirrors on the walls, but trying to see anything with six guys crowding around was impossible. Lise knocked on the door. "Two minute warning," she called.

The girls' second number started as we plastered our faces with foundation, brushed mascara onto our eyelashes and applied the eye shadow.

"How do I look?" asked Ryan

I grinned at him. "You look great!" He really did look great. All the guys looked great.

Around the room the guys surveyed each other. Lise knocked again. "Let's go knock 'em dead," said Neal.

We filed out of the room as the girls' music ended and had just lined up behind the black curtain when they appeared out of breath. Valerie giggled. "You made it."

"How do I look?"

She had a quick look. "Fantastic." Then she frowned. "Did you put lipstick on?"

My hand darted to my lips. "Oh no, I knew I forgot something." The guys were starting out onto the ice and I could hear the laughter of the crowd.

"Never mind," she said. "I'll fix that." And she pressed her lips against mine. "Good luck," she whispered while the guys pulled me along.

I was still reeling from the touch of Valerie's lips on mine as I skated out onto the ice, but the roar of the crowd pulled me back into the arena. I searched the stands for Dad and Lise, but all I could see was a blur of laughing faces. We really were quite a sight. "Get moving," muttered Carl behind me, and I looked up to see the other guys skating daintily across the ice behind Neal.

We skated into position and picked up the hems of our skirts. That was the cue for the woman who was manning the music machine. From behind the glass, the girls cheered us on. I glanced nervously at Ryan as the first few bars of music played and a hush fell over the crowd. Could we possibly pull this off?

The first few line manoeuvres were simple ones in groups of four and the crowd was more than generous with their applause. The whole building sounded like it was going to come down the first time we lifted our skirts and tossed our feathers. By the time we got through our footwork sequences and into our block formations, the crowd was clapping so hard we could hardly hear the music. The V intersection went smoothly, our feathers just brushing each other's shoulders. We were really getting into it — dipping our feathers, wiggling our hips and trying to look seductive when we were supposed to. We looped into our concentric circles and again the crowd went wild.

We were winding up now, into the most difficult part, the rotating wheel move and the music was really picking up. I grabbed onto Theo's shoulders and started the wheel formation while the group on the outer edge of the circle skated into place. Then we were there, all of us in a three-spoke wheel. All that was left was the big finale — a series of cross-rolls and twizzles before we did our fancy wiggle waggle and spin. Dave caught my skate on a crossover, but I managed to stay upright and then we were spinning, our skirts flying high above our shoulders. We dug our blades into the ice as the music stopped and lifted our arms into the finishing position.

The crowd jumped to its feet and screamed. And in typical hockey fashion, we jumped all over each other, our skirts flying, our voices laughing with utter elation.

It took us about ten minutes to clear the ice, having to take at least five or six bows, but when we did, the response from the girls was even better. "You guys were awesome!" exclaimed Valerie leaping into my arms. I hugged her close and then leaned back and kissed her, once on the lips and then on the lips again.

All around us, the guys and girls embraced, celebrating an incredible feat. The Falcons had just pulled off a synchronized skating number.

"Could I have your attention, please, your attention please." The master of ceremonies was on the ice introducing the novice pairs. We made our way to the dressing room.

Knowles joined us a few minutes later, shaking his head and laughing. "I never would have believed it, if I hadn't seen it," he said. "Maybe you guys are in the wrong sport."

Someone threw a hockey glove at him and we squeezed out of our dresses and stockings. "You're supposed to leave your dresses on the hooks. One of the mothers will collect them later." He paused and grinned. "That is of course, assuming that we're still going to play, ladies." He left the room.

We changed into our hockey gear. The Zamboni would be out to clean the ice following the figure skaters, so we had a few minutes. Getting our costumes off was easy enough, but the makeup was a little tougher. "Can you imagine having to wear this stuff all the time?" asked Pete, scrubbing at his face.

"Not!" retorted Geordie. "It feels like plaster."

By the time Knowles came back, we were all in our uniforms and lacing up skates. He launched into the game strategy and filled us in on our opponents. Phil Keefler had put together quite the team, with four ex-NHL'ers and lots of old junior players. We were going to have to out-skate them if we were going to generate any offense. "Whatever you do, don't try to get fancy. These guys have moves that most of us can only dream of," said Knowles.

Someone knocked on the door and we filed out. The black curtain had been removed and the crowd was just returning to their seats. "Ryan," called Knowles from behind us.

Ryan stepped back into the corridor and I heard him gasp. He grabbed his mother's hands and looked proudly at his dad who stood behind her. Mrs. Davis looked happier than I'd seen her look for a very long time. "She really enjoyed your last number," said Ryan's dad. "We both did."

"Why didn't you tell me Mom was coming?" Ryan beamed at his dad.

"I wasn't positive. I didn't want you to be disappointed if she didn't make it."

Ryan squeezed his mom's hands. "We've got to go," he said, looking over his shoulder at me.

His mom smiled and although I couldn't explain it, my heart soared. I punched Ryan on the arm and tore out onto the ice.

Maybe it was the fact that his mother was here for the first time in a very long time. Or maybe it was the excitement of just having pulled off a synchronized skating number and received one incredible embrace from Taryn. Whatever it was, Ryan was flying from the word go. He tore around the rink in warm-up, blasted shots past Geordie and urged us on like we were playing an overtime period, and the game hadn't even started yet. But his enthusiasm was infectious and by the time we got to the bench, we were pumped. Knowles took one look at the lot of us and grinned. "I don't think you boys need a pep talk," he said. "Let's go."

Our line was out first with Ryan centreing against Phil Keefler. They smirked at each other from behind their cages. Phil won the faceoff without even looking down and the game was on. Knowles had been right. They had moves that we could only dream of and twice I got left standing, watching my man break for the net. One of those cost us a goal by Hap Hansen, only three minutes into the period. The crowd clapped appreciatively, but I got the sense that they were really cheering for us. The girls certainly were.

"Don't worry about that goal guys," said Knowles encouragingly. "They're going to be strong for the first little while until the conditioning factor sets in. Make them skate with you."

That's what Red had intended to do, but getting past Frank Butler's stick was something else. "One little jab and it's gone," complained Red on the bench. "The guy's probably twenty kilograms overweight now, but he doesn't even have to move to take the puck away."

Ryan motioned me forward towards the faceoff circle. We were in their zone and I knew that he was thinking we might be able to get a quick shot away. I leaned into the opposing forward and Ryan, quick with his stick, managed to pull the puck away from Eric Donovan. I one-timed it, letting it rip. The puck rang off the goal post. A terrific "Ahh!" escaped from the crowd and then a tremendous roar. I looked up to see the light on and Ryan's fist in the air. He had put the rebound in. Ryan was on me before I could even stand up and the game was tied 1-1. The noise was deafening.

The referee finally made a special request for quiet and dropped the puck. Phil was out and again he won the faceoff. But the play was whistled down on the offside right away and Phil and Ryan faced off again. "Your head," Phil whispered as he squared off opposite Ryan. "Don't forget your head."

I saw Ryan glance up and then, still staring at Phil, take the faceoff. This time he was much closer, forcing Phil to draw twice to clear the puck. We did a better job of making them skate and the play went end to end for about three minutes before we got the whistle.

"Nice job guys," said Knowles. "Force them to skate like that for two periods and I guarantee you they won't have legs left in the third."

We watched as Red's line got a shot on net, but their goalie was quick with his glove hand.

"Who's in goal?" Theo wanted to know.

"Walter Matthews. Used to play junior hockey," Knowles said. "He's good, but nothing extraordinary. Keep shooting. Something will go in eventually."

But nothing else got past Matthews in the first period. He looked solid, but then again so did Geordie and we filed out with a 1-1 tie.

"Our opportunities are going to come in the third period, as they tire," Knowles insisted on his way out of the dressing room. "Just keep it simple for a while and bide your time. If we get out of this next period with a tie, you can consider yourselves to be in a good position."

We gulped mouthfuls of Gatorade. "That's what he thinks," muttered Pete. "I promised Jolene at least a one goal lead going into those final five minutes."

"Simone wants a minimum of two," said Neal.

"That's a big order," murmured Jared.

"Especially without the stuff." I cringed at James' voice.

"I thought it was good for a couple extra days," muttered Pete.

"Never mind that," advised Ryan. "Let's just get out there and show those old men what we can do."

"I second that!" I said, glad to have the subject changed. "No grandfathers are going to show us up."

Neal banged his stick on the dressing room floor and the rest of the guys joined in. When the knock on the door came, we were ready to go.

And go we did. Jared managed a quick shot from the slot, but it wasn't enough to get by Matthews. Back came the Old-timers, but Tony intercepted a pass at centre ice and went in with Red on his wing. Red blasted one, but it was just wide.

We changed on the fly, with Ryan, Justin and I jumping the boards and turning on the wheels. Knowles had told us that we were going to have to out-skate them and that's what we were intending to do. It was working too. After a while, some of them fell back a little and relied on their sticks more. But not Phil Keefler. Halfway through the period, Phil deked Ryan and sent a beautiful shot over Adrian's stick into the upper right hand corner. 2-1 Old-timers.

Ryan was already on the bench when I arrived. "Tough break," I panted.

"I should have seen it coming," said Ryan.

A cry went up from the crowd and I looked up to see Dave trying to stuff the puck in under Matthews' pads.

"We're getting the chances, boys," Knowles told the bench. "Just keep the pressure on and something will go in."

For the next ten minutes, we did just that. We could tell that they were tiring, but although most of the play was in their end, we couldn't turn that light on. "Geez," I complained to Neal on the bench, "every time you think you've got a clear shot, some yellow jersey shows up."

"I know. I had two shots deflected out there."

Knowles slapped our shoulders. "It just takes one, boys, just takes one."

Our line went on with a minute and twenty seconds left in the period. Ryan won the draw and sent it in my direction. I shot it through the winger's feet and caught Ryan who was driving hard to the net. But the puck skipped and rose off the ice. Ryan thrust his stick out in front of his body and deflected the puck. Matthews had been screened and didn't even know it was in. The crowd let him in on the secret. 2-2.

"Not quite the way I'd imagined it," Ryan muttered as we clambered back onto the bench.

"Who cares?" said Red. "We'll take it."

"You bet we will!" I exclaimed. "It's about time we had a little bit of luck."

"Let's hope it lasts," murmured Scott as Hap Hansen let one go and Blaine Petersen moved in for the rebound. Geordie managed to bury the second one and we all breathed easier. The referee dropped the puck just as the buzzer sounded to end the second period.

Knowles was ecstatic. "Great hockey, great skating, great passing." He clapped his hands. "You guys are in a great spot going into this period. Already, they're starting to slow down. By the end of the third, they're going to be dragging and all your young legs are going to be skating circles around them."

Geordie swallowed a mouthful of Gatorade. "Don't give them the blue line. Once I get a bunch of bodies in front of the net, it's tough to see."

The rap on the door came earlier than expected and we filed out for the third and final period. The crowd was really getting into this game and I'd never heard such an ovation as we stepped onto the ice. I caught a glimpse of Dad hollering. Lise was having a quick word with the referee and I could imagine how nervous she must be with this whole weekend depending on the fire alarm. The ref nodded and grinned. I figured everything was a go for the last five minutes. But the girls were counting on us to give them a lead going into those final five. They roared as we skated past their section and headed for our players' box.

"Skate, skate, skate," instructed Knowles. "This is when you'll see the age-youth thing really become a factor."

Ryan lost the first faceoff against Phil Keefler, but we fought back. Adrian intercepted a pass and took it into the Old-timers' end, but he couldn't get a shot away. They were tiring, but they were still solid on their defence and good with their sticks. And they were obviously trying to slow the game down, passing more often in their own zone, looping around in the neutral zone and blasting it into the corners unless they had a walk-in shot. We weren't used to that style of hockey and it showed.

Knowles called a time out six minutes into the period. "You're playing right into their hands," he explained. "You've slowed the game down to their speed. Go after them, badger them when they try to pass and keep your sticks out in case you get that interception. Make them play your game. Don't play theirs."

His words rang in my ears as I watched Neal, Dave and Pete skate out for the faceoff. But it wasn't so easy. Their passes rang true and it was hard to get a steal.

"We can't play cat and mouse out there," Ryan said, as we waited for the change-up. He glanced up at the empty stands where the girls had been sitting. "We don't have time."

It was true. The girls were, right now, getting changed, listening for the thunder of the crowd to indicate that we'd scored. Ryan was right; we had to do something now.

And we did. Our next shift, Ryan managed a hard wrist shot. A loud gasp went up from the fans. Matthews was down, but the light wasn't on and the puck was nowhere in sight.

The referee whistled the play dead and slowly Matthews shook himself out. No puck. The defenceman poked Matthews' old skates. The puck had lodged between the blade and the sole of the skate. I couldn't believe our bad luck.

Our bad luck was their good luck. Phil Keefler's line came out sailing. Ryan and I watched from the bench as Geordie stopped two quick shots, but Theo and James were having trouble clearing the puck. James sent the puck rolling around the boards and their defenceman managed to keep it in. He faked the pass and let go a shot that found the top left hand corner. 3-2 Old-timers.

Five minutes and twenty-two seconds left. I looked desperately at Ryan. It was going to take a miracle to give the girls even a tie to work with.

Miracles don't happen in twenty-two seconds. But well-laid plans do. Before the ref could drop the puck, a uniformed cop approached him. The ref promptly skated across the rink to talk to Knowles. "It appears that your vehicle's parked in a handicapped parking zone, coach. The officer here would like a word with you."

"A handicapped zone?" Knowles sputtered. "I didn't park anywhere near one. I'm in the middle of the second row."

The referee shrugged. "He seems pretty determined. You might want to speak with him so he doesn't have your car towed."

Knowles swore quietly under his breath. "Can't he just wait a few minutes?" he asked gesturing towards the clock.

At that precise moment, Turnbull shuffled around the arena to the bench. "Everything okay, here?" he asked.

I glanced around the rink, looking for Lise, but I couldn't spot her. So far, so good, except we were supposed to be out in front by now.

"Some crap about me parking in a wheel-chair zone. I've got to go talk to the man in blue over there. Think you could take over for a few minutes?"

"Sure," said Turnbull, "but make it quick, eh? You're not leaving me in a good spot here."

Knowles swore again and half-slid across

the ice beside the referee. We could see him speaking to the officer, obviously pleading his case, but the officer wasn't having any part of it. Our minds weren't really on the game, but we managed to hang in there for twenty-two seconds until the fire alarm blasted. In moments, the intercom was directing people to the emergency exits and Turnbull was hustling us into the dressing room where the girls were waiting.

CHAPTER 18

The girls were already dressed, with their hands over their ears to ward off the noise. Valerie hollered something at me, but I couldn't make out a word of it. I pulled off my jersey and handed it to her. It was dripping with sweat and although I couldn't hear what she said, I was pretty sure by the expression on her face that she was not impressed.

The fire alarm stopped ringing just as Lise burst through the door. "Everybody ready?" she asked.

"I guess so," said Karen, adjusting Scott's jersey. "Except you didn't tell us how smelly these uniforms would be."

Lise held the door open. Neal put an arm around Simone's shoulders and said what we'd all been dying to say. "It would sure be nice if you could pull off a tie."

"Sure thing," said Karen sarcastically. "What chance do old NHL players have against a team like ours?"

"I thought you might have some secret weapon we don't know about — some female plan," said Neal hopefully.

Taryn tugged on Valerie's arm. "Maybe we do," she said, as Lise ushered them out onto the ice.

We had strict instructions to stay in the dressing room, at least until the play started, but within seconds we could hear the laughter of the crowd. By the time the referee had dropped the puck, we were all plastered against the glass. Julie took the faceoff, or made an attempt to, against Phil Keefler. She swiped at the puck and caught his skates, sending him crashing to the ground. The crowd howled with laughter and the girls disintegrated into fits of apologies and giggles.

The ref whistled down the play and tried it again. The Old-timers had control of the puck, but it was pretty obvious that they were a bit unnerved by the whole situation. They skated around in the neutral zone, throwing questioning looks at each other, while the girls skated towards them en masse. I groaned as Valerie, Kristie and Julie attacked one offender leaving the others open for a pass. But the Old-timers had underestimated the girls' speed and they soon found that they had to pick up the pace a bit to avoid being caught. The crowd, sensing that there was a remote chance that the girls could actually do something, started to chant and the girls played with more enthusiasm than ever.

"Positions, positions," screamed Knowles, sprinting around the arena on his way to the bench. He stopped in his tracks when he saw Neal. "What are you doing here?" His voice trailed off as he caught sight of the rest of us. We stared at Knowles. He covered his face with his hands. "Let me guess — you've sold your jerseys to a synchronized skating team." A slow smile spread across his face. "Well, let's see what you taught them," he said, leaning against the glass.

Carol was hollering at Karen to come off the ice, but she was engaged in what appeared to be a serious conversation with the ref. Finally the referee nodded and she skated off, giving Taryn and Valerie the thumbs-up sign. Less than two minutes remained. The Old-timers won the draw and seemed content to pass the puck around in their zone, rather than shoot on the poor girl in net. After all, all they had to do was protect a one-goal lead, and it didn't look like that was going to be too difficult. The girls were moving well out there and even playing positions once in a while, but every time the puck ended up on one of their sticks, their heads went down and they lost it. "A little more stickhandling technique might have been a good idea," said Knowles.

The Old-timers moved in and Eric Donovan raised his stick like he was about to shoot, but the crowd booed so loudly that he shot the puck round the back of the net instead. Taryn picked it up and carried it up the rink. "Yeah, go Taryn," Ryan screamed, as we all marvelled that she'd managed to cross two lines with the puck still on her stick. The Old-timers were collapsing into their zone, giving her some room, when Valerie went charging across the blue line and collided head on with a yellow jersey.

In what seemed like slow motion, her body spun around, her stick flung across the ice and she went down, her helmet slipping off her head and her long brown hair fanning over the ice. The crowd held its breath and I leaned against the glass. "Get up," I whispered under my breath. "Get up."

Hap Hansen, whom she'd collided with, was already kneeling on the ice. The other Old-timers circled and skated back to the scene. Even Matthews had thrown back his facemask and was halfway to Valerie when Dave jabbed me in the ribs.

Coming across the blue line was Taryn, skating casually past the retreating yellow jerseys, her eyes focused on the puck. The empty net stood in front of her and she hugged the boards to pass Matthews before turning towards it. She looked up and then with almost the right amount of wrist action, let a shot go. It rolled across the goal line and the light went on. An enormous cheer went up from the girls' bench and a bewildered Old-timers' team looked around as Valerie jumped to her feet, threw her hair back over her shoulders and skated down the ice to join in the hugs of the other girls.

And suddenly it all clicked. The whole thing had been staged. The referee had never blown the whistle to end the play. We joined in a round of high fives as the referee signaled that the goal stood and the scoreboard registered a 3-3 tie. The crowd stamped their feet and hooted and even Knowles had to admit that he'd never seen so much ingenuity on the ice. It took almost five minutes for things to settle down and when they did, all eyes turned to the clock. Twenty-six seconds remained.

We held our breath as Phil Keefler and Hap Hansen lined up. Karen and Jolene were on and both of them could really skate, but it would only take one shot. The Old-timers were biding their time, setting up the perfect play, so they'd only have to shoot once. They passed it back and forth in the slot while the girls panicked, running from one side to the other. Then with the countdown at eight, Hap Hansen shot, a quick wrist shot to the side. Karen took one look at his stick and jumped, straight into the puck. The ref whistled the play down with two seconds remaining.

Once again, the arena held its breath. Phil Keefler took the faceoff and shot. It went in, but the buzzer sounded first. It was a tie and we had the girls to thank for it. We stumbled out onto the ice, hugging the girls and shaking hands with the Old-timers. Beside us the crowd was on their feet standing and the roof threatened to fall from its rafters. Somewhere in that screaming throng, Lise was smiling.

It was quite a while before Lise managed to get the girls out of the dressing room. Nobody, not even Carl, was in much of a hurry. Knowles stopped in once, reminded us that our game against the Cadillacs was Monday at 7:30 sharp, and left chuckling.

By the time Ryan and I made it into the lobby, someone had erected a large sign declaring free pizza for all today's participants at a local pizzeria tomorrow evening. I caught sight of Valerie with her mother and headed across the lobby.

"And this must be Joel," she said as I came up. "I believe I spoke to you on the phone once." She smiled a warm, amused smile while I turned red. "What a wonderful performance you boys gave today."

I felt the colour creep further into my face. "Thanks," I said. "I guess you saw Valerie in that tying goal?"

She nodded. "I did. I think I'll sign her up for drama next year."

Lise came up behind me. "Joel, sorry to interrupt." She glanced up at Valerie's mother. "Lise Harper-Swystun — I'm Joel's stepmother," she said, extending a hand.

"Yolanda Sherman, I'm Valerie's mother."

Lise smiled. "And I finally get to officially meet Valerie."

Valerie nodded and I watched in amusement as she blushed scarlet.

"I assume you two are planning to attend the pizza celebration tomorrow?" Lise said, indicating the sign in the lobby.

I looked up at Valerie. "I'll be there. How about you?"

Valerie glanced up at her mother. "I have to work," said Mrs. Sherman. "Maybe you could catch a ride over with one of the other girls."

"We can pick her up," Lise added quickly, before I could even ask, "and bring her home too. It's no problem, right, Joel?"

I smiled at her. "No problem at all."

"All right then," said Valerie's mother. "Thank you."

"We'd better go, Joel. Dad has to meet some clients this evening."

"It was nice meeting you," said Mrs. Sherman. "And the showcase was brilliant. I understand you were part of the organizing committee. You did a superb job!"

I studied Lise. She was wearing the patch-work sweatshirt I'd given her for Christmas and she was beaming. She looked great.

"Definitely," agreed Valerie.

"Awesome!" I said, meaning it.

Lise inclined her head towards me. "Thank you," she said, meaning it too.

I said my good-byes and joined Dad, who was standing with Ryan at the doors. "Where's your mom and dad, Ry?" I asked.

"John took Ryan's mom home," answered Dad. "She was so tired that she was almost asleep on her feet." He smiled from me to Ryan. "I think she laughed harder than any of us."

I watched Ryan who couldn't stop smiling. He'd been right. He hadn't stopped believing in his mom and he'd been right. Exiting the arena that night, I couldn't think of how things could get much better.

But Sunday was just as good. Ryan called around noon to tell me he'd been up to see his mom and she was better than she'd ever been. She'd even talked to him. And Lise picked up Valerie, Ryan and Taryn that night. It was our first double date and we were two of the happiest guys in the world, walking into the pizzeria with our girls on our arms. Valerie was all mine that night and making no attempt to hide it, and I couldn't get enough of it.

Everything was perfect until Neal caught me on the way out the door. "Hey Swystun, what about the stuff. We have to play the Cadillacs on Monday and this last batch won't still be working by then," he whispered in my ear.

I motioned towards Lise and the girls standing in the doorway. "We'll talk later," I said, but somehow my perfect night had been ruined.

"Did you have a good time?" Lise asked as we drove home.

"Yeah," I murmured, "up until the end."

"Valerie?"

"No, the guys wondering about the stuff." I leaned back against the headrest. "I know, I know," I added before she could say anything. "But it's not going to be easy."

CHAPTER 19

The guys were all over me at lunch the next day. "Did you bring it?" asked Pete, sliding onto the bench beside me.

"To school?"

"Well, when are we going to get it, then?" Pete lowered his voice. "We need it tonight."

Just then Valerie slid in beside me. "Need what?" she asked.

"A focused hockey team," answered Ryan from across the table. He threw me a meaningful look before heading off to buy a chocolate milk.

"I can hardly wait," said Valerie.

"You're coming?" I asked, leaning closer to her.

"Are you kidding? We all are. Wouldn't miss it for anything."

Theo grinned. "Oh great, our own cheering section. Will you be in your uniforms or kimonos?"

Valerie stuck out her tongue at him.

I laughed, glad of her company and the opportunity it presented to avoid the subject of the stuff once again. I even managed to sneak away early after school, when my Science teacher dismissed us with five minutes to go, but I knew that the moment of truth would come soon.

I delayed as long as possible getting ready for the game, but Lise finally pushed me out the door and into the car. "Come on," she said, "just get it over with."

"You're going to tell them tonight before the game, aren't you?" asked Ryan as I waited for him to get his shoes on.

"Guess so." What choice did I have?

Ryan slung his hockey bag over his shoulder, then reached for another blue sports bag.

"What's that?" I asked as we headed out the door.

"Just some stuff."

We joined Dad and Lise in the car. "Are your folks coming tonight?" Dad asked Ryan.

"Dad went to pick Mom up. They'll probably be a little late."

We were a little late as well, but Knowles hadn't put in an appearance yet. I could see the questions in the guys' eyes as soon as I walked in. "All right," I said, putting up one hand, "I know what you're going to ask and there's something I have to tell you." I took a deep breath and glanced over my shoulder at the door. "There's no more stuff."

The guys erupted. "Oh man, how could you do this now, Swystun? This is our big game."

"The game of the season and we have to go without it!" groaned Justin. "We're going to get smoked."

Ryan put two fingers to his mouth and let out a shrill whistle. "We are not!" He stared hard around the room. "We don't need the stuff to play great hockey."

"Like you can talk," said Justin. "It hasn't hurt your game, has it?"

Ryan grabbed the blue bag and hauled it out from under the bench. His face was dark and determined. As he bent to unzip it, Taryn and Karen burst through the doors with the rest of the synchronized skating team behind them. "Okay, I know we're not supposed to be in here, but we figured maybe you guys could use these," began Karen. She held up a box of red garters. "They're our good luck garters and we wore them at provincials this year, and well, we won."

The sight of the girls squished tightly in the doorway, holding up a box of garters, was too much for us. Neal started to laugh and soon we were all roaring. Red took a garter and put it on his head like a headband. Geordie wore his over his eyes and made some comment about not having seen the puck, and Tony wrapped his around his biceps twice, like he was in mourning. Despite the comments, each of us took one and managed to work it into our uniforms. After all, hockey players are highly superstitious.

The girls were just clearing out when Knowles walked in with Phil Keefler and another short, wiry man. "Okay," began Knowles dubiously, as the last of the girls exited and we tried to hide the bright red silk garters. "All of you boys know Phil Keefler." We murmured our hellos and tried not to stare at the box in Phil's hands. "Mr. Keefler has a generous gift for the team."

Knowles left with the short, wiry man while Phil stepped forward. "Once, many years ago, I played in a world hockey tournament against the Russians," he began. "I was lucky to have a chance to get to know one of the best players the game of hockey has ever seen. Some of you may remember Sergei Makarov."

We breathed in unison. He had been hailed as one of hockey's all-time greats, before he'd been killed in a car accident in the prime of his life. Everyone knew of Sergei Makarov.

"Well, the season before he was killed, he visited me when he was playing here in Canada. Just showed up one night at my home, carrying this box." Phil opened the box carefully and pulled out a bronze falcon, its talons extended, its beak open. "Inside were two of these birds. Sergei's father had made them as good-luck talismans." He paused, remembering, while we sat silent. "He gave them to me that night. He said that I reminded him of a falcon on the ice — smooth, fast and always watching for an opportunity." Phil stroked the bronze bird's shimmering tail feathers. "He said they would bring me luck, that his father would make him another good-luck talisman. They did bring me luck over the years."

We sat, staring at the falcon — the ripples of its feathers, the slightly open beak, the glint of its eye.

"I've kept one as a keepsake, but I want you boys to have the other one. After that game on the weekend, well, I know how much this game today means to you, and I thought you could use a little luck. You're a real decent bunch of kids." He handed the falcon to Ryan who cupped it in his hands. "Give it a rub, before you go out on the ice. It worked for me."

We murmured our thanks in whispers, completely awed by the gift in Ryan's hands. Phil Keefler cleared his throat and continued. "And boys, if you ever want to play good hockey, today's a good day to do it. The little guy that was just here with me, that's Tom Dreyfus. He's a scout for one of the junior teams. I know that's a ways off, but a little recognition now could go a long way in the future." He left, leaving us in silence.

"I guess you know what's on the line," said Knowles as he wrapped up his pre-game speech. "You boys have a chance to score big today, real big." He glanced around the room. "So let's get out there and show them how to play hockey."

Ryan placed the falcon on the blue sports bag in the middle of the room. "Yeah," he breathed, "let's play hockey."

One by one the guys filed past the falcon, stroking its powerful back and wings. Finally, only Ryan and I remained. I cupped the bird with my hands, feeling its strength and speed surge through me. Then I handed it to Ryan who held it tightly, his eyes closed. He placed it gently back on the bag and followed me out the door.

My skates hit the ice surface in the midst of a wild cheer from the stands. The girls were on their feet, screaming. Phil Keefler and the scout sat in the next section, examining some papers.

"Hey Swystun," called Knowles as I skated by, "where's your visor?" My hand went instinctively to my face, only to realize that I'd forgotten my visor.

I raced back to the dressing room, grabbed my visor and was about to leave when I saw the bronze falcon. As I picked it up, its talon caught the zipper and pulled the bag open slightly. Inside were dozens of clear packages containing a fine white powder. I put the falcon down and drew the zipper all the way back. Ryan's Sinus Minus — his entire stash. None of it had been touched. I'd known Ryan hadn't taken it since his injury, but I hadn't known he'd gone all season without it.

I zipped the sports bag up and threw it under a bench. Then I raced back down the corridor and out onto the ice. I took a couple of hard laps then lined up beside Ryan on the blue line. "You never took it, did you?" I asked as Dave teed up the puck and let a shot go.

Ryan looked up in surprise. "Just that first time at Pete's house." He stopped the puck on his stick. "I couldn't, Joel, not after everything." He let a hard shot rip and found the five-hole. "After that night at Pete's — well, it scared the hell out of me knowing how easy it had been."

"And you brought it tonight so the guys would know that you'd played all season without it . . . that you didn't need it . . . "

" . . . and neither did they," concluded Ryan.

I caught a pass and let a good shot go into the upper corner. "How come you never said anything about me giving it to the guys at the beginning?" I asked, joining Ryan at the end of the line.

"I knew you'd sort things out." He grinned his trademark grin. "But it sure took you long enough."

The whistle blew as Ryan's words hit me. He hadn't given up on me, just like he hadn't given up on his mom. Lots of other guys would have. But he'd believed that I'd find a way to set everything right. And I had. I glanced towards Phil Keefler and the scout as Ryan skated towards the bench. If I had anything to do with anything today, Ryan would be talking to that scout after the game.

Ryan stared hard at Keller across the faceoff circle. He'd only played a few games since his rib injury, and I knew from the look in Keller's eyes that the Cadillacs thought he had a weakness. But there was nothing weak about his faceoff skills or his moves. Near the end of our shift, the two defencemen moved in to sandwich him, but Ryan cut hard to the left, then the right. The defencemen collided as he deftly swept around them, banging the shot into the upper right hand corner of the net.

I gave him a high-five on the bench. "Nice move!"

Ryan grinned. "I've got a few more that I'm dying to show them."

I'd never seen him skate so well or outmanoeuvre so many players in my life. By the end of the first period, he'd managed five shots on goal and Horvath was sweating. However, despite our efforts, and a power play opportunity, we were only up by one when we skated to the dressing room.

Knowles was cautiously optimistic. "You guys are looking great out there. Davis that's the fanciest bit of skating I've seen for a while.

Must have been that synchronized skating you did." The guys laughed. "Nevertheless, these are the Cadillacs, and they're not about to concede the game after one period. Remember, don't take any unnecessary penalties. We don't want to make it easy for them."

The guys nodded and guzzled fluids.

"They're going to be looking to slow the game down and give themselves time to set up. Keep it quick and watch for the open man. They'll be all over Davis this next period, so you forwards will get some more opportunities. Use them." Somebody knocked on the door. We pulled our helmets back on.

I glanced up at Tom Dreyfus in the stands and then across at Ryan. Coach Knowles had been right. The Cadillacs were hitting, playing the man instead of the puck. I got nailed near the Cadillacs' blue line and looked up dazed.

Ryan had the puck behind the net. He skirted it along the boards to Theo who fired from the point. The rebound deflected off a skate. Somehow Ryan managed to come up with the puck and passed it back as Smithers checked him. Adrian fed it to me and I skated hard, sidestepping a check and laying it onto Justin's stick. His quick wrist shot turned the light on. 2-0 Falcons.

We crowded around the bench, congratulating Justin until the ref blew the whistle and play resumed. The Cadillacs were shuffling their lines and Knowles was changing on the fly trying to match them. One of their defencemen got a good shot away from the point. Geordie handled it easily, dropping it around the back of the goal for Neal. But the red jerseys were right on top of him. Neal tried to pass to Pete, but Keller intercepted it just outside the slot and Geordie didn't have a chance. The scoreboard read 2-1 Falcons.

"Don't worry about it boys," advised Knowles. "It looks like they've decided to play hockey, and that's what we're here to do."

The play raced from end to end. We changed lines frequently, trying to keep the legs out on the ice fresh. The Cadillacs were playing it tight, making it hard to freewheel. Scott lost the puck in the neutral zone, swung off the check and tripped the winger with his stick. The ref whistled it down and the Cadillacs went on the power play.

Keller won the draw, and set up on the blue line. Alex intercepted a pass and popped the puck back into the neutral zone, but the Cadillacs just regrouped and came at them again. This time they went in on a three-on-two. Alex and Tony did their best, but Smithers tucked it underneath Geordie's pads and suddenly the game was tied, 2-2.

"We need one," murmured Ryan, circling me before moving into the faceoff circle. "Soon." He won the draw, ragged the puck and put a sensational move on his man, before charging for the goal. Horvath was screaming at his own players to clear the slot, and they did, forcing Ryan to drop the puck back to Justin and skate towards the boards. Justin sent it back to Ryan just as Renegade pummeled him. Ryan went down hard on top of the puck. The referee signaled for a penalty.

While Keller argued with the ref, I skated over to help Ryan up. He pushed himself to his feet and winced. "Your ribs?" I asked anxiously.

"No, my funny bone."

I laughed with relief.

Neal, Dave and Pete went out for the power play, and managed a few shots, but nothing with any intensity. With twelve seconds left, our line went back out against Keller's. Ryan took the faceoff in the Cadillac zone, won the draw, spun around and shot. I sat dumbfounded as the light came on, almost as dumbfounded as Horvath.

"Is that a Phil Keefler trick too?" I asked, pounding his helmet, as the period ended in a 3-2 score.

"You can't play defensive hockey," Coach Knowles told us in the dressing room. "There's still a full twenty minutes left. You've got to stay on the attack. One goal could turn this game around."

Keller was shadowing Ryan, trying to keep him out of the play. He'd done it in previous games, but this time Ryan was shaking him off with some fancy footwork. Alone in the Cadillac's zone with the defencemen, he looked around. I crossed the blue line, banging my stick to let him know I was there. He stopped on a dime, made a blind pass and

I blasted a shot at the goalie. Horvath went down on the first save and Ryan popped the rebound high for a goal. The guys mobbed him, congratulating him on his hat trick. Seventeen minutes remained and we had a two-goal lead.

The Cadillacs called a time out and we used it to catch our breath. "Don't sit back," advised Knowles. "This is a big game and they're going to use every trick in the book to get back in it."

Knowles was right. And not all those tricks were on the up and up. The elbows were being used more than ever and the sticks were being carried higher than usual. Jared took a knee in the groin and limped to the bench. Neal went out in his place and immediately got flattened at centre ice by Renegade. The crowd screamed, but he'd been checked behind the play and the referee hadn't noticed.

I could see Neal looking for Renegade. They went around behind the Cadillac's goal together and again Renegade hit him hard, jamming his helmet into his back. Neal turned around, his stick in two hands and charged. It was exactly what the Cadillacs had hoped for. A retaliation penalty.

Ryan and I went out to kill the penalty. Ryan ragged the puck and iced it, but Horvath came way out of his net and sent it back into the neutral zone. The Cadillacs pressed hard, but we succeeded in getting a whistle in our end with only twenty seconds remaining in the penalty. Scott lost the draw and Keller put on a burst of speed. He skated hard for the net, faked a slapshot and left it for Smithers who blasted it past Geordie. The red light flashed and suddenly it was a 4-3 hockey game.

"Whatever you do, don't retaliate," screamed Knowles. "We're still up by one. They're looking to use that power play."

Knowles was right. It was obvious from the first faceoff when the centre stepped straight into Ryan without even making a move for the puck. Ryan spun away and the Cadillacs scrambled to set something up in our zone. I stole the puck, took an elbow in the chin and another in the ribs before laying a pass onto Ryan's stick just as Renegade moved in. Ryan cut hard, changing direction. Renegade fell.

His stick caught Ryan's skates and sent him smashing to the ice on top of the puck. The ref gave Renegade the benefit of the doubt and nothing Neal could say would make him change his mind.

"Where'd he learn to referee?" demanded Scott. "At the Cadillacs' school of refereeing?"

The guys were pretty riled and the Cadillacs knew it. I saw O'Neill skate by Scott and whisper something to him. Scott's head jerked up and fire flashed from his eyes. The Cadillacs won the faceoff and went on the attack. Our guys dropped back to defend the net. Bodies collided in the slot, and suddenly, fists were flying and helmets were bouncing across the ice.

Knowles jumped onto the boards and ordered us to remain seated. Out on the ice, blue and red sweaters rolled about as the black and white jerseys charged in. Eventually everyone was separated and all the gloves and sticks picked up. We huddled around the bench and waited. The ref was at the box assessing penalties. We'd both lost two players to game misconducts and we were a man short. One minute fifty showed on the clock.

Coach Knowles rallied us for the final short-handed shift. "They'll probably pull their goalie as soon as the play moves into our end, so be prepared. Now's not the time to lose a faceoff, Davis. Then skate with the puck. Don't be afraid to ice it, but make sure you get it out."

Ryan won the faceoff and circled around the neutral zone as their goalie, Horvath, skated off to the bench. There were six Cadillacs to our four, and they came at us hard. I tried to ice the puck, but it hit a stick, bounced into our zone and the Cadillacs set up. Theo and Adrian stood their ground while the Cadillacs managed one, two, three shots on Geordie. Ryan stole the rebound, pulled the puck in close to his body and wove through the red jerseys, spinning off a check and breaking clear, puck intact, into the centre ice area.

The noise in the arena was deafening as Ryan turned on the wheels, out-skating the winger who was racing from the opposite side and letting a wrist shot go into the empty net. Twenty-four seconds remained on the clock.

On the bench, I pounded Ryan's back as Red's line went out for the final shift. Even Knowles jumped down and hugged Ryan, then me, then Ryan again. The buzzer sounded and the roof lifted off the arena. Only then did I remember that the girls were all there cheering us on.

We hoisted Ryan onto our shoulders and took a victory lap. It took quite a while to get the guys calmed down enough to shake hands. I helped Ryan collect his equipment that was strewn about the ice surface. "Mom's here," said Ryan as we passed the stands.

We skated towards the gate. Coach Knowles was standing there with Phil Keefler. With them was Tom Dreyfus, staring at Ryan. Who could turn their back on a performance like the one Ryan had given today?

"Swystun, Davis," called Coach Knowles, as we reached the gate. "Come here, boys." We stepped onto the black rubber where Phil Keefler stood with Tom Dreyfus.

My heart thumped loudly as Tom extended a hand to Ryan. "I'm Tom Dreyfus. You played a first-rate game today." Ryan shook the hand.

I fought the urge to scream with happiness — for Ryan, for his brilliant play today, for his mom, for the chance to make his dream a reality.

"I was hoping you might be able to join me for dinner tonight, along with your folks. I think we've got a few things to discuss."

I slapped Ryan on the back and he found his voice. "I . . . I'll have to check with my parents," he said quickly. "They're right here, in the arena." He moved forward, his eyes gleaming as Phil Keefler stepped down to embrace him.

I watched them, wanting to shout in elation. Coach Knowles nudged me and I reigned my emotions in. Tom Dreyfus was staring expectantly at me. "Pardon me?" I muttered, feeling that I had missed something. Coach Knowles chuckled.

"Do you think that would be possible, Joel?" asked Tom again.

I stared blankly at him.

"Dinner, tonight with your folks, to discuss things?"

I nodded, my eyes widening, my lips moving but no sound coming out.

"All right!" screamed Ryan, suddenly leaping past Tom Dreyfus, wrapping me in a huge bear hug and knocking me off my feet.

The men laughed. "I'll ask your parents to come down," Coach Knowles told us.

Ryan pulled me to my feet. "Can you believe it?" he whispered, suddenly overcome by emotion.

I grasped the shoulders of my best friend. "Ryan," I began, trying to find the right words. "Thanks for . . . well . . . thanks."

Ryan grinned his trademark grin. "I must admit, I was beginning to wonder." He pulled me down the corridor. "What was it anyway?"

I smirked at him. "You don't want to know."

"Sure I do."

At the end of the corridor, I could see Coach Knowles talking to Lise, Dad, and Mr. and Mrs. Davis. I snapped my fingers and chanted, "Stuffed up and sneezy? The solution's easy. Doesn't matter if you're young or old . . . "

Ryan joined in for the last line. "Just mix up Sinus Minus, and throw away your shyness. For a healthy sinus, minus the cold."

AGMV Marquis

MEMBER OF THE SCABRINI GROUP

Quebec, Canada
2001